Reviews

"Pappin has based his story on two topics widely highlighted in recent times, but set them in the mid-1950s. Schoolyard bullying and deceit and underhand machinations in local government are certainly subjects worthy of examination. Although at first glance these may appear to be two widely differing areas of concern they both are about bullying by the stronger and the better connected. Thus one can see these as problems which have continued to beset our society.

The author has taken these two areas of concern, for many today very emotional, and skilfully intertwined them around the fictional Daraleeth River, the lifeblood of Bowater. Here in the verdure of north-eastern Victoria, life for many of the citizens of the Bowater Shire has many problems. The main characters are very well portrayed, their connection to the main thrusts of the story well illustrated, and the reader is readily able to accept the final outcomes. The author is highlighting very important topics for us today.

— Glen Natalier, author of *Healing in the Holy Land* and *Sunrise in the West*

For Whom The River Runs is a wonderful story ! It's the kind of book that you want to get comfortable with and just sit and read without any disturbance. So well written, the story flows delightfully and the characters are completely absorbing. Life in the country town is so beautifully described that you

will feel you live there too. Heart- warming and feel good, it was so enjoyable. The last few chapters are quite magnificent. Recommended reading. Congratulations to Wayne F A Pappin for a great read from start to finish. "
— Alison Lewis, author of *Missing* and *Seasons of Life*

"A poignant insight into the lonely life of a young boy crippled by Polio, and his best friend who is mentally scarred by his heritage. Their desperate longing to be accepted by their peers leads to tragic consequences. A nostalgic reflection of friendship and growing up in an intolerant society."
— Vivian Waring, author *When Tears Ran Dry*

"The star of this novel is the author's vivid descriptions of how life was at that time. So vivid in fact, you can actually believe you are there with Peter and Aadje, trying to escape the continual harassment of the bullies to just live their lives in relative peace.

"I urge any history loving reader to read this book of friendship and loss; memories and regrets. Australia as it was then seems a completely alien place to our modern world now but the author's vivid writing skills makes this novel a 'must read'."
— John Morrow's *Pick of the Week*

FOR WHOM THE RIVER RUNS

A Novel

Wayne F. A. Pappin

Published in Australia by Sid Harta Publishers Pty Ltd,
ABN: 46 119 415 842
23 Stirling Crescent, Glen Waverley, Victoria 3150 Australia
Telephone: +61 3 9560 9920, Facsimile: +61 3 9545 1742
E-mail: author@sidharta.com.au

First published in Australia 2019
This edition published 2019
Copyright © Wayne F.A. Pappin 2019
Cover design, typesetting: WorkingType (www.workingtype.com.au)

Pappin, Wayne F.A.
For Whom the River Runs
ISBN: 978-1-925230-61-1
pp210

ABOUT THE AUTHOR

For Whom the River Runs is Wayne Pappin's first novel. The unfinished manuscript lay dormant for many years. Work and family commitments meant the draft struggled to see the light of day. Now retired, and with more time on his hands, the author, in a flurry of determination, decided to drive the spectre of procrastination from the desk top of failed ambition and finish the manuscript. The incentive was to leave something by which his children and grand-children would remember him.

The author began his working life as a Secondary School teacher, then as an Electorate Officer for a Member of Parliament and, before retirement, was, for over five years, the Associate Director of a large Faculty at a Victorian T.A.F.E. College. Variously he has been a Councillor on the City of Whittlesea and is currently very active in the local community and a member of many committees.

For my loving wife Delma. My three talented children, Tamara, Caitlin and Nicholas, their partners and all my delightful grandchildren.

The author thanks his editor, Barbara Ivusic, for all her support and skill in massaging and fine tuning the manuscript into its finished format.

An Echo in Time

Peter Devereau sat absorbed with his tribute to a long-lost friend. It was the twentieth anniversary of his death, and, as he pondered the words he had penned, his mind danced back to a time shrouded by the mists of long ago. A time serrated in discord and etched with tragedy. A tale of dashed hopes and of a lad challenged by forces most unforgiving. The saga of a town divided on itself and of a rural idyll in search of redemption and beset with the ripples of power, intrigue and mockery. With his muscular arms, Peter Devereau adjusted the braces on his withered legs and reached for his walking sticks. Rising, he shuffled to his front window and, while gazing out onto the jacarandas playing sentinel in the street, reflected on his mate, and of that one year in paradise lost.

A reflection which staged two decades of drama and passion across the theatre of his being. The window's glass pane crafted an image that framed a resolute soul whose blue eyes spoke of tenderness and dogged stoicism. With a shake of his head, he ran his fingers through his shoulder length hair and mused that he had come a long way and had experienced much in the last twenty years. At the age of sixty-three, failing health had forced his father's early retirement from the Shire of Bowater. When, he, along with Peter's mother, relocated to the more temperate climes of bayside Williamstown. Following Aadje's passing, Blackie and Ginger, wracked with guilt, salved their conscience by befriending him with regular fishing expeditions and some adventures to savour. A stint at RMIT qualified him as a journalist and, after working as a copyboy, secured a job with the Bowater Bugle. To spite his disability, he learned to drive and met his future wife while covering the political aspirations of the local candidates during the 1972 Federal Election campaign. A campaign, like others before, in which political evangelists on a civic mission elevated self-promotion and hubris to an art form and who wrapped the stark realities of power and privilege in shrouds of subterfuge, denial and arrogance. The winds of change were in the air and this excited the good burghers of Bowater into fits of apoplexy. Whitlam supporters in the bush were few and far between and those that were, kept their own counsel lest they offend conservative sensitivities and raise the ire of the ruling elite. Peter Devereau had been forged in the crucible of adversity and shaped by the politics of his day. Vietnam and Whitlam scripted his existence as surely as his callipers. The blocking of supply and the recent defeat of the Federal Labor government left an indelible mark on his spirit. He mourned the method of its passing and bemoaned the lost opportunity to create a dominion where justice and equality were its creed and crowning glory.

Turning from the window on callipered heel, Devereau paused awhile at the sepia and framed photograph of a boy and his faithful dog. A whimsical smile creased his bearded features as he slowly returned to his writing desk. With roving eye, he sadly scanned his opus to a mate long gone. It had been a January day, much like this one. A sweltering sun had baked a landscape brown, a shimmering haze of purgatory that bleached the very soul and banished mercy's child to the house of the Devil.

'I miss you my friend,' whispered Devereau, lost in the shadow of his memories. Catharsis near complete, he signed off on his eulogy with a flourish. As a journalist, he rued its lack of classical lustre, but took comfort, as all scribes should, in its fidelity and found solace in the thought that his mate would understand.

'This is for you comrade. May you rest in peace.'

Ode to Aadje
Aadje Kuiper, his spindly frame he hoist,
A pivot of shaky resolve, a brow so clammy moist,
Onto the top rail o'er the chasm Daraleet,
Murky depths, from perch to water all of thirty feet.

Dappled shadows caressed its span sublime,
The setting sun, a golden orb of ambience divine,
A January twilight, all placid and serene,
And of a boy's pale and slender body, halo'd as the scene.

Uncertainty and confusion came flooding by,

Tethered in fright to some perilous eyrie up on high,

Reality a'sobered with sweated palm and knotted fear,

A mind in torment, a will to yield and frailty so near.

The jagged cramp of strain and seduction,

Carried the sinews of the flesh to the edge of destruction,

From the souls of the feet to his very essence,

There below the abyss lurked, ghosted by a fiendish presence.

The mired waters that swiftly flow, beckoned with tendrals deep,

He bravely plunged, arms a'stretched and honour for to keep,

From lofty height, with strength and grit he plummeted in descent,

The shadowed void ruptured deep, a symphony echo'd in torment.

The river in all its might and mocking mirth,

Drew the young man to its foaming girth,

Its peace and tranquillity veiled a sinister bite,

That snatched poor Aadje from his dreams and put them all to flight.

Aadje leap'd with daring, martyred in innocence and purity,

That spurn'd Lucifer's worst in rhythm and riffs of clarity,

T'was much too high a price to give and much more for to pay,

To showeth for all to heed and fable, that he was as good as they.

Peter Devereau

With a shrug, he put aside the tribute to his friend and to the lilting refrain of Kris Kristofferson's, *For the Good Times,* he again found himself trekking through the hinterland of his past. As nostalgia strummed its melancholy chord, the echoes of his memory bounced back to early 1955. When tragedy prowled the landscape and stirred the dust of misery that spawned this wretched tale.

Pilgrims All

P eter Armstrong Devereau pushed aside his breakfast plate, prised his legs free from beneath the kitchen table and locked his callipers into place. The stainless-steel splints bracing his legs and the walking sticks leaning against the back of his chair were trophies, constant reminders, of a virulent attack of poliomyelitis which left both legs atrophied and weak. Devereau, with one hand on the seat of his chair and the other on the table, levered his body to its feet and with an awkward swivel reached for his metal crutches. Using the laminex table for support, he took his satchel from his mother and wrestled it onto his back. Gripping the crutches with their metal elbow supports, he clumsily made his way down the long passage to the front door. Peter, with his callipers locked and his walking sticks under control, was at least independently mobile, even if somewhat slow and ungainly. His mother preceded him down the passage and wiping her hands quickly on the ever-present apron, the universal uniform of motherhood, opened the door.

'Have a good day at school son. You do as you're told and come straight home, alright,' were his mother's parting words.

'Yeah mum,' was Peter's practiced and indifferent response. The verbal shrug of the shoulder, a commitment well meant, but made with a tone of flexibility. Peter had heard these words virtually every day since he could make his own way to school. And this, the first day of term two proved to be no different. His mother, if nothing else, was a creature of habit.

Bowater Higher Elementary School was three quarters of a mile away in Bowater West. Peter had been at the school one term after starting in February. His father, William Devereau, at forty-one, had been appointed to the Bowater Shire Council as its new Shire Secretary and had relocated his wife and then twelve-year-old son lock, stock and Ford Prefect in early January 1955. A day that seared their memory while baking them to the core. A day etched deep into the conscious of the Devereau clan. As far as Peter and his mother were concerned, Bowater and the bush were the creation of a cruel and mocking mind, with the scorched and shimmering backdrop a fitting stage for Shakespeare and all his tragedies. A landscape, in which Hamlet and Lady MacBeth could sweep eternally through the stubble hacking with sword and dagger at a sea of troubles, their own guilt and everybody's despair. That summer was blistering. The heat belted from the baked and yellow land, while a relentless sun crushed the life out of everything with an intensity that made the trip north to

Bowater a trial none of them would ever forget. The Devereau Ford overheated, Peter's mother overheated, Peter dehydrated and the head of the Devereau dynasty cursed his stupidity in applying for, and his bad luck in gaining his new title as Bowater Shire Secretary. His Presbyterian God had created Heaven and Earth in six days, Bowater was obviously the Devil's contribution. 'This bloody place is hotter'n hell,' was all that William Devereau could mutter, stating the obvious to no-one in particular. His wife, at every utterance, glared at her husband of sixteen years and said nothing with a silence that stroked his guilt and burned his very soul. The sweat poured from his crimson face in torrents, his shirt and pants clung to the car seat and his hands, wet with perspiration, felt alien to the steering wheel.

The long drive, a violent sun and yellowed stubble stretching to the far horizon, wilted their spirits and hammered a deepening wedge of anxiety into their very being. When the family of pilgrims finally struggled into Bowater, population 2,200, or so the welcome sign read, the relief was audible. Peter's father had only visited the town once for his interview and that was by train during the late spring of '54. A day bathed in warm sunshine and calibrated in comfort. It took a few impatient minutes to navigate the town, find the Shire offices and park the now internally haemorrhaging Ford. While the new Shire Secretary, shirt ringing wet and caked to his back, dragged himself up the bluestone steps of the Town Hall, Peter and his mother slid from the car and flopped on the grass verge beneath the sheltering umbrella of a date palm. Peter and his mother did not care how long it took his father to collect the keys to their future home, the longer the better. That palm was a bit of paradise and after a hell of a pilgrimage, they had found something akin to heaven. Neither of them was in any hurry to leave it.

On that January day, William Devereau abandoned his wife and son to the palm's tender caress and cool embrace while, with sweaty fingers, he pushed open the large wooden door that stood vigil as the entrance to Town Hall. With all the surety he could muster, Devereau disappeared through the hallowed portal that was local government. Inside, the mahogany portico cast the sombre, conservative shadow of authority. Unstated, but writ large on the psyche of all who enter this municipal vault is the aura of power and its halo of sovereignty. In front, the counter, polished to a shine by a myriad of transactions and errant elbows, was neatly labelled: '*Rates; Enquiries; Water Board and Pound*'. A municipal clerk, high on his wooden perch and with a signature scowl common to those afflicted by failures of ambition, observed through narrowed eye lids, Devereau's transgression against municipal sanctity. On the wall and behind the wooden barricade that shielded the clerk from the vagaries of a world daring to invade his sacred sanctum, were the flags of state and the realm, together with the ornate crest of the Shire of Bowater. Flamboyant in design, the shield in hues of green and gold promenaded the image of sheep and cattle, framed by crossed sheaths of wheat. All embraced by a motto whose genesis reflected the mantra of governance, enterprise and optimism: '*Fauci-tus per Operati*'; Prosperity through Toil. Above all, was the newly commissioned portrait of the nation's reigning monarch, Elizabeth Windsor, Queen of the Empire. Devereau welcomed the cool embrace of a foyer with its thick brick façade, high ceiling, parquetry floor and strategically placed wall fans blowing waves of relief over his heated being. Quickly taking in his surroundings, he noted that to the left of the clerk's station, and behind closed doors, he could hear the clatter of keys manipulated by an unseen typist of consummate skill. To the right, were the double doors of heavy mahogany clearly marked '*Council Chamber*'. Directional signs at the base of wide, varnished stairs heralded the existence of the '*Engineer*', '*Health Inspector*' and '*Valuer*'. As testimony to their status as slick gears in a machine of perpetual motion, they were exalted inhabitants of lofty roosts in the second storey.

Opposite the Council Chamber, Devereau made out a large panelled door with a frosted glass insert imperiously stamped, '*Shire Secretary*'. Devereau allowed a smile to rimple his face and, in spite of himself, basked in the sweet nectar of success and hubris. As reward for his own good fortune, Devereau managed to take two steps towards his new personal edifice when the clerk, in a pitch that brooked no recalcitrance, asked. 'Can I help you?'

Devereau, abruptly brought back to reality, explained that he was the new Shire Secretary and was here to pick up the keys to the Council house which came with the job.

Humbled by the spectre of dominion, the clerk's tone softened in acquiescence.

'I'm sorry. We weren't expecting you until later this afternoon Mr Devereau. We were hoping the Shire Engineer would be here to meet you when you arrived.'

'I left the city early to miss the heat. That obviously didn't work. It's hotter than Hades out there.'

'It'll get hotter yet,' was the clerk's laconic and thinly veiled response.

'Do you mind if I have a quick look at my office?' asked Devereau.

With an ambiguous nod that lacked commitment, the clerk, on grabbing some keys from a drawer somewhere within the bowels of his counter, slowly made his way to the panelled door and, without fanfare, pushed back the last impediment to Devereau's quest for the Holy Grail and municipal grandeur. The vista, orbed in summer hues, framed a somewhat cramped office resplendent with an expensive, large wooden writing desk and a swivel chair in lush green leather. The walls were lined with bookcases filled with copies of various Local Government Acts and Council Minutes detailing the intricacies and history of the Shire of Bowater. A refrigerator, a wooden filing cabinet and small conference table took up the remaining space. Devereau stood and drank in the future of his existence. Forcing down a rush of enthusiasm that stroked his ego and exalted his achievement, he, with all the respect he could muster, thanked the clerk and gently closed the door behind him, leaving the ruffled clerk to make his own way back to his counter. Devereau rolled back the lush desk chair and, on sitting down, pondered over the complex of responsibilities he had inherited as Shire Secretary of a rural community. A community, rich in conservative values while firmly mired in the shadows of its English heritage. With one last scan of his new-found diorama of authority, Devereau, on closing the door behind him, re-entered the foyer and asked the clerk for the keys to his new dwelling.

'They're with your office keys. It's the one with the green dot on the shank. There is also a spare key if you need. The address is 13 River Road, across the railway line and to your left. Just follow the river,' instructed the clerk

'The removalists got the key yesterday and moved your things into the house. So, it should all be ready for you.'

'Thanks for your time. I start in the job tomorrow and I'm to meet the Shire President and some staff in the morning at nine o'clock. I'll probably catch up with you then.'

'I'll be here,' were the clerk's parting words to a disappearing Devereau. For what he lacked in enthusiasm, he more than made up for in clarity.

Devereau sauntered down the bluestone steps and stood for a time gazing up at the edifice of municipal sovereignty and its two stories supported by Doric columns that framed its bluestone and brick façade. In the park adjacent, stood the granite War Memorial to fallen soldiers and a flag pole draped in the flag of the realm held limp in the absence of a breeze.

The Council house the Devereau's inherited along with their new role in municipal affairs, was most welcome, not only for the relief it offered, but it signified the end of a journey that had its heat-soaked genesis some five hours before. It was near midday when the faithful Ford finally pulled up at the front gates of the bagged brick California bungalow, with its hipped roof and brick pillars supporting the portico verandah. The house sat squarely on an expansive block, with plenty of shade trees and oleander bushes. A row of roses stalked the gravel driveway to a garage on the edge of wishful thinking at the rear of the block. A large area of grass masquerading as lawn fanned out from the front and back, all captured within a perimeter fence of cyclone wire and timber. To the front, River Road boasted an avenue of jacarandas that corralled its gravel surface and dusty footpath. It was clear from the state of the property that Council staff had maintained the garden, keeping it trim, tidy and well-watered. Given the former Shire Secretary had departed a month before, it was more than Devereau had hoped for. The transition, comparatively seamless, owed much to the good management and determined efficiency of Council in expediting a replacement for a Shire Secretary whose quest for a soft billet and longevity had overwhelmed his capacity for effective governance and community service. As expected, the removalists had dropped the personal effects into the hallway of the sparsely furnished house. As Mrs Devereau busied herself unpacking linen, crockery and family keepsakes, Peter embarked on a purposeful, if somewhat ungainly tour of his new place of abode. He missed his Northcote friends, but welcomed his new-found wide-open spaces and a garden full of trees. While, spectacularly simple, the California bungalow accommodated all that is associated with a three-bedroom cottage, including a toilet majestically parked at the end of a well-worn path some twenty paces from the back door. An outhouse in all its glory, heralded by a faded shingle on its door proclaiming, 'Thunder Box'. The handiwork of a mind steeped in the art of trespassing against good taste. William Devereau, having disembarked the last of the family's valued artefacts from the trusty Ford, joined his wife and son under the shade of a willow myrtle for some tea and biscuits.

'Tomorrow is a new dawn,' he thought. 'I'll relax right here this afternoon and ready myself for the challenges that must surely come.'

CHAPTER TWO

Discord in Arcadia

The morning was chilly as Peter shuffled his way down the path and out the front gate on his way to begin a new term at Bowater Elementary. His withered, callipered legs made for ungainly slow progress as his pronounced limp kicked up puffs of dust on the formed track that doubled as a footpath. Having just turned thirteen, Peter had lived with his disability and the frustration attached to his walking stick props for as long as he could remember. Over time and with encouragement from all quarters, Peter, through bouts of anger, self-pity and will, mastered the art of mobility that spited his iron legs. He was at least mobile, pendulum like, where his legs were swung forward while they waited for his crutches to catch up. While ungainly to the eye and frustrating in restriction, Peter Devereau was at least perambulatory with some level of independence and sense of purpose. His was an iron will that matched his legs of steel.

Peter's circumstances presented limited opportunity for him to actively participate in the rigours of sport and develop friendships with the more robust students at Bowater Elementary. His isolation, compounded by the absence of acceptance and practical empathy by those deemed to be his class mates, caressed seclusion and introspection. Breaks found him playing a lonely tune where his only company was the silence of his own laughter. Then, one lunch time, in late February, another of Bowater Elementary's misfits gravitated into Peter Devereau's joyless trajectory and filled the void of friendship so elusive to both. Aadje Kuiper was a year older than Peter and was ostracised by the local toughs, not because he was disabled, but because he was different. Aadje Kuiper, while conceived in Bowater, was the product of Dutch immigrants. Ridiculed for his ancestry and spindly frame, he was derided for his lack of sporting acumen. He wore, mockingly, the mantle of the impoverished and was bullied as an unwelcome contagion on the space rightfully belonging to those whose Anglo heritage gave them sovereignty over Bowater and all who reside therein.

Peter and Aadje came together more by accident than by design. The loneliness of the school yard snares kindred spirits as they drift aimlessly in search of acceptance and companionship. Peter was drawn, first by the jeers and then to a forlornly scrawny lad who was the butt of the insults. Harassment knows no bounds in the skilled hands of a bully, and Aadje was powerless in the face of overwhelming and stronger odds. With quivering lips his response was mute as, racked with shame and failure, he scurried away from his tormentors. To the lilting chorus, 'clogs, clogs. You're nothin' but a dirty dog,' Aadje found sanctuary behind the shelter shed and out of sight of the school yard ruffians' hell bent on making his life a misery. It is in this orbit that Peter first met the object of their derision. The two welded by circumstance and tarnished by imperfection, had become close, with each keeping the other company. A shield against the vagaries of a world that they felt was so uninviting. A sanctuary and shared cocoon, where they were protected from the barbs of outrageous fortune and all its injustice, bigotry and aggression. Peter and Aadje made their way home from school together as far as Curlin's Bridge, whereupon Aadje crossed, heeled hard right and headed for his house on the outskirts of town. Peter then continued the quarter mile to his own home rich in the solitude of his own being. Each morning, so long as Aadje felt up to school, they met at the base of the bridge for the half mile journey to the nemesis of their adolescence. Curlin's Bridge, named for Major Curlin, who, in the 1840's, leased forty-two thousand acres of prime country for the grazing of sheep and cattle. The run straddled the Daraleet River and gave rise to the settlement that morphed into the current town of Bowater. The good Major made the leasehold secure by driving off the original inhabitants whose fire power was no match for the carbine, rum and disease. The bridge, at its apex, stood some thirty feet above the river's russet waters as it snaked its way north to the vibrant pastures of the Murray-Darling catchment. The Daraleet, the conduit to prosperity and Bowater's salvation, was a ribbon of verdure cutting a swathe through a parched and barren hinterland. Curlin's Bridge, iconic, revered and denigrated in the same breath, was, with stealth, exploited by the town's young bucks in a reckless test of bravado and the search for acclamation. Success was surviving the half-pike executed from the wooden handrail into the turgid deep below. It had, through myth and tradition, become a symbol of manhood via a risky and heroic rite of passage.

For Aadje, the trail to Bowater Higher Elementary meant crossing over the Daraleet, its lurking menace cloaked in serenity, and trekking along gravel footpaths to the school. Saluting in turn, the Co-operative Milk Factory, the local parish church, the Mechanics' Institute and the recently established bowling club, which glowed verdant in its new-found prominence. Gum trees of various hues formed an avenue of embrace for the eager young faces as they funnelled their way to school. For Aadje and Peter, this journey to school on the first day of the new term was like all others. A pilgrimage filled with mock bravado. They talked, they cajoled and they laughed as they masked a new season of discontent through a mix of deflection, bluster and jovial camaraderie. This morning Aadje was dressed as he was last term when the sun lingered with the last warmth of spring. His shirt was frayed at the collar, faded blue shorts and tattered jumper complemented his battered shoes which lacked the adornment of any semblance of socks. His school uniform, while clean, lacked the refinement that comes with money and telegraphed a family struggling to make ends meet on a widow's pension. A family alienated from the rewards made real through the beneficence of a significant bread winner.

In his short life, Aadje and his mother, Anki, had worn their share of tragedy and despair.

Aadje's younger sister by two years was cruelly stricken with a virulent attack of double pneumonia and was buried a week after his ninth birthday. Aadje's father Geert, who, with his new bride, escaped the gathering war clouds of Europe by immigrating to the sundrenched land down under. A land far from the travails of a Europe mired in the grip of impending turmoil. It beckoned with outstretched arms and the promise of hope and security. His exodus, propelled by the chill winds of foreboding was tinged with guilt and regret. A melancholy compounded in jettisoning family and heritage and an unease in abandoning his native land to the forces of fate. With Holland's near neighbour flexing its expansionist muscle and with lebensraum as its mantra, Geert and his wife left the old world to its best devices and hurriedly exited south.

Having arrived by steamer in Melbourne in early 1939, Geert found work in the heart of north central Victoria at the little town of Bowater. He and his wife secured a cheap and modest, if somewhat dilapidated, home on the outskirts of the township in Bowater East. Trained as an electrician in his native Holland and with English adequate enough to gain employment, Geert joined Bowater's newly established McAlister Electrics as a *sparky*. An Australian idiom, a bemused Geert embraced as his new occupation. Geert's arrival and employment in Bowater was fortuitous given that electricity supply had only brightened the township since the middle of 1937. Growth in electrification provided opportunity for the industrious and gave Geert a solid start in his adopted country. Not long after their arrival and while Europe was in the grip of war, the Bowater Bush Nursing Hospital welcomed Aadje in 1940 and his sister, Dagmar, in 1942. For Geert and his family, Bowater, with its quiet isolation, quarantined them as a safe haven while the ravages of conflict consumed the nation and its young fighting men. War was a world away and Geert worked hard in the best European tradition to provide for his family and to absorb and embrace the cultural normality of a small country town. For Geert, the rural idyll was the high altar of salvation, peace and serenity. He had settled in Arcadia and embraced its tender mercies. Life was good. At war's end, Geert had established himself as a hard-working family man on the cusp of middle-class respectability. While residual suspicion still lingered over this European interloper, with his strange accent, perceived arrogance, cultural mores and vague religious orientation, he was, if not entirely welcomed, at least accepted. He and his family had made in-roads into a small community wary of strangers, fearful of progress and steeped in the conservative Victorian values of church, hard work, community and obedience.

The death of his only daughter in 1949 sent Geert spiralling into a chasm of grief, from which, some say, he never recovered. While carrying his burden of bitter sorrow with stoic resolve, Geert silently railed against the world, his God and the Bush Nursing Home for their duplicitous failure in rescuing his beloved daughter from the darkness of the abyss. Despair snuffed, just three years later, in a shower of sparks and flame. While working on a sub-station at the local cannery, Geert, in what many claim was carelessness brought on by deep sorrow and familiarity discharged 240,000 volts through his soon to be lifeless body. Geert died instantly as he was hurled twenty feet to the ground in a crumpled, smoking heap. Half of Bowater lost power in that instant and, with all the unexplained premonition of a wife's canny instinct, Anki Kuiper sank to her knees, fearful of the worst.

Aadje, deeply saddened by the death of his father, missed his dad dearly. But, in the intervening three years, the drift of time and the vagaries of youth had cauterised the pain to ebbs of nostalgia and longing. His mother, forged in the furnace of migratory hardship, steeled herself against the dark tentacles of fate, made most of her anguish, shook the branch of the Devil's worst and made the best of it. When money ran short, Anki took in washing and, with Aadje's help and her heavily accented English, made a determined, if somewhat meagre, path through the brooding morass that had been visited upon her and her family. Anki's widow's pension, together with the menial task of washing for the privileged, just managed to keep food on the table and pay the bills. The small amount of compensation she received on Geert's death was long gone. His funeral had seen it evaporate into the grave and headstone that marked his demise.

Bowater Higher Elementary, with its brick façade and freshly painted portico, stood out as a beacon of learning and spiritual enlightenment. Since its genesis in 1923, it has become, next to the church, the place where young minds are fashioned in the conservative mould of God, country and obedience. Where sports toned the body and the classroom coloured the horizon. The school is the beating heart of Bowater, with Bowater the centre of all creation. A Garden of Eden charged with disseminating power and the glory throughout the cosmos. Its students, an eclectic mix, replicated the social structure and class divisions of the region. A kaleidoscope of the wealthy, the average and the lowly battler swarmed through its hallowed gates in search of salvation, acceptance and liberation. The narrow path through the cyclone wire gates, corralled by rough cut grass impersonating lawn, provided the quintessential gauntlet as the sheep wended their way to their lockers and onto class.

As Peter and Aadje, with all the anonymity they could muster, made their way along the path, the giggling of the girls in front was silenced by the taunts of half a dozen older boys, ably led by Aadje's nemesis, Blackie Gavin.

'What's the matter, clogs? Can't you afford decent pants. Look at your skinny legs, Kuiper. You are as weak as water,' bellowed Blackie for the world to hear.

'Yeah! You're a sissy. You're scrawny little runt. Go home to mummy,' chorused Blackie's support crew of mindless Neanderthals. While Peter and Aadje scrambled up the path, eyes cast vacant to shield them from any further ill-will, the jeering faded to a cacophony of girls laughing and boys yelling. Once more, left in the splendid isolation of the ignored, they moved as quickly as Peter's shrivelled legs could propel them to their lockers. The corridor laid in polished linoleum, buffed to a pattern-less sheen, was long and narrow. Banks of lockers stood sentry its entire length and the autumn sun streamed through the head-high windows and bathed the lockers in preordained halos of light. Aadje's battered school satchel gorged its frugal contents into his locker. The two jam sandwiches, a dry biscuit, a shard of scrap paper and a pencil was all he could contribute to his enlightenment. Lunch for Aadje, as was generally the case, erred on the side of his mother's available income. It was dependent on savings from her pension and how much washing she took in.

'Is that all you've got to eat?' queried Peter, whose lunch boasted fruit and cake.

'I'll be right. It's all I need for today. I'll eat when I get home,' was Aadje's less than committed response.

Amid the ruckus of banging lockers, dropped books, raucous laughter and the rhythmic clang of the school bell, Aadje and Peter made the slow, but familiar trek to school assembly. Peter, of suspect dexterity, carried his school work in his shouldered satchel which gave his arms the freedom to manoeuvre his crutches. The nimbler of his brethren carried their work books in cradled arms that bespoke of an affection, more superficial than felt.

Battalioned up in class lines, Aadje in Form 3 and Peter in Form 2, the entire cohort of uniformed pawns in search of academia faced the flag of the Commonwealth and stood at silent attention as the Head Master began to speak. Flanked by the two school captains, the Head Master instructed his charges, so assembled, to salute the flag and recite the Oath of Allegiance. An oath, so well-rehearsed that its meaning had been lost in a welter of repetition and irrelevance. The Head Master informed his captive congregation that two teachers, one art, the other music had left the school over the break and would not be returning for term two. He, with a glance that spoke of enlightened retribution, relayed to the assembled multitude that the Deputy Head Master would fill the breach and teach art until a replacement be found. The Deputy's blank expression belied some previous indiscretion. Music, the Head Master intoned, would not be taught until further notice. With that, the assembly concluded without further admonishment.

'Assembly dismissed. Move quietly to class please,' was the practised, if firm, direction from the paid oligarch who ran the school as a duchy and all his charges mere vassals forged in the cauldron of learning. Students regimentally, two by two, marched off to the strains of *God Save the Queen* and followed their teacher, like leashed lemmings, into the corridors of knowledge. Aadje, whose class is anchored parallel to Form 4, invariably, and by sinister design, found himself too close to Blackie Gavin and his mates for pleasantries. Aadje endured the slings and arrows of Blackie and his acolytes all through assembly as they whispered snide and jeering insults from the corners of their clenched mouths.

'We'll get you after school, clogs. So, watch out. We're comin' for ya,' were their parting words of warning.

Aadje, questing for solitude and security, galvanised his scrawny frame and made haste after his teacher and into the protective embrace of his classroom.

The forces of bias had mobilised against Aadje and moved like a phalanx of malice from the time Blackie and his knaves had determined that he didn't measure up to their ingrained notions of physical prowess, social status and ancestry. At every opportunity, Blackie, together with his fellow merchants of menace, stalked Aadje with a passion born of superiority and fanned by the zephyrs of boredom. For the two years Aadje had attended Bowater Elementary, and since leaving primary school, this was his lot, with his only refuge being the protective bunker of class and the shelter of home. Break times saw Aadje willing himself invisible and, in inheriting the mantle of the damned, kept out of sight. Not until Peter arrived at the school three months ago did Aadje discover solace in the company of the spurned and the isolated. Peter, with his callipered legs and small physique, was of no value to Blackie and his support crew. Whether that be on the playing field, or as the butt of snide innuendo and mocking harassment. Peter's physical travails, so pronounced, so open, were off limits even to Blackie and his truculent minions. The black heart of the bully finds its own level of darkness and where the light shall not bear witness. It attaches to the challenge arising from the affliction of misery. Peter, with his burdens of steel and ease of prey, was too profound a difference to stroke the enjoyment of Blackie and his vacuous consorts. To do otherwise, risked earning the collective ire of all they deemed to impress. Poor Aadje, on the other hand, was just like them, only weaker, smaller and more vulnerable. Harassing Aadje was the vehicle of choice. It steered their quest for power, self-esteem and school yard respect, camouflaged weakness and massaged their egos.

For lunch, as it had been all year, Peter and Adje hid, entombed, behind the timber walls of the shelter shed. It was their very own barricade, a shield against the adolescent injustices of a cruel world. Aadje's lunch, as was common, was frugal to say the least. While offering him a home cooked ANZAC biscuit, Peter, in all innocence asked. 'Why do those kids pick on you Aadje?'

'I dunno,' was the sighed response. 'Me dad was Dutch and I guess they don't like Dutch people who can't play football,' was all Aadje could offer. They ate the rest of their lunch in silence and, in unison, rolled over to watch the clouds pirouette through the serenity of their heavenly embrace. They observed the scudding clouds, a montage only broken by the joy, laughter and yelling of youngsters at play.

'I wish I was a cloud,' Aadje intoned, basking in the peace and tranquillity of his elusive dream. A fantasy jarred to reality by the clanging of the bell that heralded the end of lunch.

As was his practice, Aadje, by instinct and self-preservation, plotted from a distance Blackie's trajectory as he, Blackie, made haste slowly back to class. Aadje could then make a dash, unseen, back to the safety of his classroom. Experience had long taught Aadje that his harassment interfered with Blackie's regular lunchtime activity of kicking the footy and sneaking a Capstan. If he kept out of sight, he was left in peace to ponder his after-school demise. There had been times when circumstance intervened to allow Aadje to bolt off home without coming across his tormentors. However, since befriending Peter, his options for escape had been slowed to the pace of the shrivelled legs and built up shoes of his one and only mate. Luck's a fortune if you already have wealth, but, this day, as Aadje was navigating the pathway and out through the gates of his torment, he ran afoul of Blackie and his minders who began to jostle and shove him out onto the roadway.

'Hey, clogs. Go home, mummy's boy. Ya gotta get the washing in you sissy,' chorused the insults that assailed him. As Aadje stumbled under the onslaught, Curly, one of Blackie's lieutenants, snatched his satchel and hurled it to the far side of the road.

'You don't need this you dummy,' assaulted Aadje's sensitivities and his chin began to quiver in anger, frustration and humiliation.

'Leave him alone,' yelled Peter with a bravado that surprised even him. Curly, a little taken aback, responded with a push and a bark of, 'shut up you cripple.' Blackie, whose black and soulless eyes glared flint, grabbed Curly by the jumper and, through gritted teeth, warned his mate to watch himself.

'Do that again and I'll deck ya,' was the unambiguous response from the young tough's Commander-in-Chief.

With that, the fracas, in spite of the weight of numbers, came to an end. Blackie and his disciples scurried off to have a smoke and roam the town in search of mischief and harass unfortunate Catholic scholars making their way home from St. Augustine's. While shaken, Peter and Aadje stopped just long enough to scoop up his dispossessed satchel and beat as hasty a retreat to Curlin's Bridge, and home, as Peter's callipered anchors would allow.

On the way, Peter, overcome by a strange feeling of euphoria, basked in a new-found glory as the righteous hero coming to Aadje's defence. 'You okay?' Peter asked.

Aadje, gazing straight ahead, said nothing. His only response was to wipe his eyes and quicken his pace. Peter, while struggling to keep up, called after Aadje and suggested they stop by the river bank under Curlin's Bridge and watch the Daraleet plot its eternal course north. Curlin's Bridge was hewed from red gum many a decade ago at a cost of five hundred and ninety pounds. A princely sum for those days. Its timber girders and beams suspended a wooden decking with handrails at hip height, penning a planked one lane surface that witnessed the passage of wagons, cattle and sheep in days gone by. The advent of the automobile added a new dimension to negotiating the bridge, where the car competed for right of way with the itinerant drovers mustering their flocks and herds from one side of the Daraleet to the other in search of sustenance. The clatter, squeaks and thumps of stressed timber and rivets heralded the crossing of cars and trucks as they made their way slowly over the bridge.

Maintained at considerable cost to the Shire, a new bridge had been under consideration for many a year. But a growing Shire had limited capacity to finance major works and a new bridge over the Daraleet remained unfunded and unbuilt. While having a sentimental attachment to the bridge, the locals whinged incessantly about its condition and capacity and was often a topic of amber fuelled debate in the bars of Bowater's four pubs. Much to the displeasure of the local constabulary and the Shire Council, the young lads of the town flaunted the law and made the most of the stalemate by diving from its top rail into the water below.

The bridge presented as a refuge for Peter and Aadje as they lay down on the grassed river bank in the shadow of its solitude. Shards of light filtered through its planked surface and danced on the ripples of the river's journey. The Daraleet, so named after one of Major Curlin's drovers who, in the 1840's, drowned near the very spot that offered the two friends respite from torment. While mustering Curlin's cattle near the river bank, Edwin Daraleet was thrown from his skittish horse and into the embrace of a river unforgiving of those who can't swim. His drowning prompted the few locals to christen the river after him. As is usual with time and tradition, the name gathered a life of its own and was, at some stage in antiquity, duly gazetted. The Daraleet, the farmers' salvation, broadens as it sweeps to the north, bringing with it seasonal floods, snags and river flotsam and attracting the usual aviary of kingfishers, egrets, cormorants, ducks, galahs and little grebes. All the while, the kookaburra, the monarch of the river, surveys its domain from lofty perches in the gums that line the river. A little upstream from the bridge is the water hole used by town folk for swimming. Bowater, so named in recognition of the river's sharp bend where the settlement began, is physically dissected into two geographical spheres, east and west. The river's eternal meandering, by force of nature, splits the town asunder, and is fate's bulwark that separates the materially endowed from the battler. The bridge, the conduit for commercial interaction, was the spiritual boundary of social status, power and influence. It was the darkened portal to Bowater East, where the disadvantaged, the inferior, the shiftless and the godless took refuge against the patronising disdain of their over-the-river neighbours. Stretched out as they were, Peter and Aadje gazed up at the bridge's undercarriage and listened to the whistles and shrieks of the abundant bird life invading their privacy.

'You know, Aadje, ya can't keep letting Blackie push you around like that. It's not right,' Peter volunteered out of nowhere.

'I know. But, what can I do? There's always three or four of them. You're my only friend and they're too big, strong and mean for me. I can't fight 'em,' was Aadje's resigned and dispirited response.

'Couldn't you tell your teachers to get them to stop?'

'Gee, Peter, do you want to get me killed? That would make it worse for me. Ya don't dob.' Aadje's sideways glance at Peter said it all and he let the matter drop. Returning to the silence of his own weakness, Peter reflected on the hopelessness of Aadje's circumstances and his own failure as a friend. It was a silence disturbed by Aadje, who, looking up at the bridge, frowned and thumped the grassed bank with his clenched fist.

'You know, Peter. The kids in this town dive off the top of this bridge when they want to show off and prove they're real blokes.'

'Christ. They could get killed or drowned or somethin'. It would be dangerous and what about the coppers?' growled, Peter.

'Don't you see Peter? That's why they do it. Blackie Gavin, Ginger and Curly did it last summer and that's why they think they are so tough,' Aadje stressed.

'Pete.' It was the first time Aadje had called him by that name and Peter basked in the comfort of knowing that Aadje must think him a true friend.

'I'm gonna do it one day. I'll show 'em I'm as good as they are.'

'You're crazy,' was Peter's only response as trepidation morphed into a stranglehold of concern.

The two friends reclined among the grass in unspoken mateship, each in thought, communing with the sights and sound of Bowater's lifeblood as it wended its way through the hinterland. After what had seemed an eternity, Aadje sat up and said, 'I better be gettin' home. Mum might want me to deliver some washing.' Peter watched Aadje lift his spidery frame and make his way over the bridge, before turning a sharp right along the east bank and head toward the comfort of his mother's love. Peter absorbed the scene and his mate's fate a little longer. Shaking off feelings of despair for his friend, he finally raised himself, locked his callipers in place, threw his school satchel over his back and, with the support of his crutches made his awkward way home. The front path to the Council cottage the Devereau's called home welcomed him with the catchy lyrics of Johny Ray's, 'Hernando's Hideaway'. Peter's mother had early on discovered Radio CCV and absorbed the latest in musical enjoyment via a Bakelite radio holding court over the fireplace. Meeting Peter on the front verandah, she asked how school was.

'Oh! Okay, I guess,' was his indifferent answer.

'You don't seem too happy, Peter. What's the matter? It's your friend, isn't it? Is he being picked on again?'

'Yeah. A little bit,' was Peter's measured response.

'Can't he complain to his teachers and put a stop to it?' It was a question only an adult could contemplate.

'He won't dob mum,' was Peter's way of terminating the hurt and conversation. Making his way through the front door, he beat a retreat to his room. After divesting his school satchel and crutches to his bedroom floor, Peter threw himself on his bed and stared at the ceiling. Alluring in its blandness, Peter drifted off into the vacuum of his mind which left no bivouac for the world and its torment.

CHAPTER THREE

Genesis

In the three months since William Devereau had assumed control of the operational activities of Bowater Shire, he had not only immersed himself in the minutiae of running his fiefdom, but absorbed, as if by osmosis, its chequered and coloured history.

Bowater's genesis saw a strewn settlement grow, overtime, into a hamlet in search of geographical expression. Sited on the bend of the Daraleet River, at its narrowest point it was the place where Curlin's drovers crossed cattle in a constant search of fodder and profit. Curlin's Crossing, as it became known, was the primitive hub of a settlement of bark huts and calico tents. The good Major, being of sound English stock, had earlier neutralised the isolated pockets of native resistance by the discrete exercise of the mantra of the powerful, that being negotiation through escalation. The strategic deployment of buckshot, rum and disease had forced the pesky native to the furthest corner of his leasehold. By the late 1850's their civilisation was complete and the occasional dropping of a steer's carcass and whisky at the camp site kept the original inhabitants in their place. A rudimentary diplomacy not lost on the growing number of settlers. Curlin, no fool, was determined to protect his cattle and growing sheep flock from duffers and poachers with spears and woomeras. Guile and force were of equal potence when it came to the taming of the native tribes dispossessed by the Major's 42,000-acre leasehold. The invasion of the colony of Victoria during the 1850's and 1860's saw the gold digger, the scruffy and the seedy join the squatter, the selector, the artisan and the shop keeper in the quest for bounty, mateship, independence and the power that wealth inherits. Fortuitously, Major Curlin, at 72 years of age passed before he could witness the splitting up of his empire. By 1872, at the time of Curlin's death from what was described as consumption, the rural leases and the bunyip aristocracy began to expire and the land progressively unlocked for small scale holdings. At which point, Bowater's historical antecedents became an amalgam of folklore and fact. Just eight years before his death, and much to his chagrin, Bowater was proclaimed a Roads District and Curlin's Crossing passed into history. Bowater, in honour of the bend in the river dividing the fledgling settlement, was, following Victoria's Local Government Act of 1874, declared a shire in 1884. By this time the township boasted a Mechanics' Institute, drapery, blacksmith, stone mason, apothecary, wagon maker, three churches and six pubs. Curlin's rural idyll and lasting legacy was ambushed by bureaucratic sleight of hand. Revenge is sweet for those who suffer the mystifying force of arrogance, indiscretion and delusions of grandeur. His anonymity was sealed following his feud with the Colonial Governor over an earlier attempt at lease creep where the good Major emancipated a further 10,000 acres of prime grazing land. A land grab, cunningly achieved by the simple ruse of encouraging his sheep and cattle to roam outside his original emirate. The Governor was not amused and, like the dingo, waited. The strike, when it came, was swift and opportune. The new Roads District would henceforth be known as the Bowater Roads District, proclaimed a Governor basking in the warm glow of retribution. A proclamation that consigned the toll roads to the dusts of antiquity, pleasing drovers and travellers alike who resented forking out their hard earned to transgress this wide brown land. Often over roads that were little better than tracks and virtually impassable during winter. At a shilling a horse and three shillings a wagon, transients welcomed the Roads Districts as salvation from penury and shed not a tear for the demise of the tollways.

The Major lived just long enough to witness the construction of a narrow tracked wooden bridge that shoved Curlin's Crossing into history's chronicle. In recognition of his past glories, and as a salve of sympathy, the new bridge was named for the town's founding father and proclaimed with a red gum sign at either end in letters bold; *Curlin's Bridge*. With the breakup of the leaseholds that imprisoned the land in the hands of a privileged few, a new class of settler invaded Bowater and heralded the rise of cropping to complement the staples of sheep and cattle. The expanding numbers of farmers and settlers pushed into the ritual domain of the grazier and the squatter and the settlement at Bowater grew into a township. In summer, a scalded plain, while in winter a landscape framed in verdure. The river, a shadowed meander, was the lifeblood of the district, whose cloistered aisles provided protection against the ravages of drought and the sins of hubris. The completion of the weir in 1896 developed a new era for Bowater, where floods were mitigated, and market gardens flourished. The railway arrived in 1872 and, together with the flotsam ejected from the gold fields, formed the catalyst for expansion and economic development. The gold rush spawned one Michael McGurk. A miner who, frustrated at his consistent failure to strike it rich in the gold fields, decided that stealing was a far better proposition than digging. As a fledgling bushranger, McGurk engaged in the odd bit of cattle and sheep duffing and, when opportunity presented, relieved unfortunate Chinese fossickers of their meagre pickings. Having modelled himself on the exploits of the notorious English highwayman, Dick Turpin, who terrorised eighteenth century England, McGurk turned his hand to bailing up a Cobb&Co. coach and liberate the gold bullion being transported to Bendigo. Mounted on his horse, McGurk blocked the deserted road and, with carbine at the ready, ordered the coach to '*bail up*'. To his surprise, his instruction was met with a porcupine of rifles, all cocked and ready to fire, poking from the coach's every crevice.

'Holy hell,' he yelled. 'I'm outa here.'

With that he wheeled his horse and galloped off into the safety of the scrub. The coach's occupants, having erupted into fits of laughter and derision, made their way into Bowater to report McGurk's indiscretion to the garrison stationed in the town. His inept exploits earned the sobriquet of 'Mad Mick McGurk'. He was elevated to legend status when on tethering his horse to the verandah post of the local state bank, he strolled in demanding cash. The bank clerk, with raised eyebrows and grinning from ear to ear, looked McGurk over and informed him that he was wasting his time.

'You're outta luck, cobber,' he said. 'Kelly's already been and long gone. There's next to nothin' here.'

Having barely finished his sentence, the only customer in the bank, a feisty 70-year-old spinster, proceeded to beat Mad Mick about the head with her parasol.

'You very naughty boy,' she yelled. 'You need a real good belting, you young layabout. Get home to your mother where you belong.'

In fright, surprise and self-preservation, McGurk, in panic, bolted out the front door and, in a single stride, leapt into the saddle of his horse. A vigorous use of the spurs encouraged the horse to flight and in the ensuring flurry of activity, the horse, still tethered, took off, pulling down the bank's verandah and throwing Mick to the ground as it went. Mad Mick, horseless and in an extreme state of agitation, took off on foot down to the river and disappeared amid the raucous laughter of the gathering crowd of onlookers. Mad Mick was never seen again and, as his escapades dissolved into folklore and myth, his exploits, embellished by time and memory, took on a life of their own. Rumour hath it that he was shielded by sympathisers until he died in a drunken haze somewhere in the bush. Fantasy affirms that Mad Mick, in the grip of alcohol-fuelled delirium, was shooting at a goanna covetous of his beef jerky when the gun fell in the fire and discharged. Divorcing Mad Mick from this mortal coil and dispatching his soul off to St. Peter who had no idea what to do with it. His celebrity was cemented with a sign over the bar of the Imperial proclaiming for all to see, 'Mad Mick's Bar' and by a publican who claimed Mick as a regular, if surreptitious, customer. Mad Mick was a constant source of amusement to the locals who appreciated his incompetence, audacity and disrespect for authority. All added to his myth by claiming to have been either a victim of, or had aided and abetted the Colony's most inept of bushrangers.

Bowater, by the turn of the century, boasted a varied mix of hoteliers, bankers, granary workers, blacksmiths, civil servants, clerics, teachers, stock and station agents, drovers and labourers. These, together with the farmers and graziers, burnished the burgeoning agrarian idyll, spawned the unholy trinity of class, status and power and heralded the ascendency of the good burghers of Bowater and the primacy of Christian conservative values. It was a coterie of privilege, where membership was contingent upon the tenets of wealth, ancestry and religion. Superiority forged in the crucible of birth and material success. The depression of the 1890's slowed enthusiasm and development. Still, by the 1930's Bowater had bounced back with the establishment of a funeral home, a cannery, grain silos, milk factory, newspaper and a wide range of retailers. In spite of the Great Depression that began in 1929, Bowater continued its steady metamorphosis into a town that, by the 1950's, boasted 2200 residents out of a Shire population of around 5800 ratepayers. Over time, satellite settlements evolved where knots of farmers and graziers huddled together in search of kindred spirit. The Federal Government's Soldier Settlement scheme added a new dimension to the district as increasing numbers of returned servicemen embraced the agrarian dream and added valour to a landscape rich in ancestry, social status and the Protestant work ethic.

William Devereau sat at his desk, lustrous with its green leather insert, penning his Council report for Monday's meeting. During the past twelve weeks he had not only abrogated control of the Shire's daily operations, but gained some understanding of the cultural, social and political structure of the district over which he presided. The majority of elected councillors were from the stratum of society best described as landed gentry, while two others were from the business end of town. Forming a conservative voting block steeped in Christian values, enterprise and prejudice. One Catholic businessman and two non-aligned independents, one self-employed, the other a civil servant made up the remainder of the nine-member council. Cyril Dixon, Shire President was in his seventies and serving a ninth term in the chair. His crumpled three-piece suit was his Council attire of choice, but the wearing of shoes without socks was the highlight of his dress sense.

'Never wore socks. Never will,' was his retort at a time he caught Devereau staring at his unadorned shoes during one of their earlier meetings. Dixon's political skills were forged with a sledgehammer, his features chiselled with an adze and any negotiation, in the tradition of the old school, was blustery, short, caustic and decidedly antagonistic. Devereau learnt early the value and security of conciliatory manipulation and had developed the cunning of a ferret when manoeuvring around issues not to the Shire President's liking. The problem for Devereau resided in the natural alliance of Dixon and three other councillors who ruled as the entitled descendants of explorers and pioneers. They protected the privilege of their class with an enthusiasm that brooked no opposition. When wedded to a close alliance with the three business-oriented councillors, the power structure and decision making within the Shire was cemented in the hands of a conservative block, which, at every opportunity, quarantined its vested interests from the unruly and the shrapnel that is outrageous fortune. Devereau had provided executive support to Council at its three previous monthly meetings and serviced a number of council committees. They were uneventful, purely administrative in function and followed the procedural guidelines of a standard structured meeting. Devereau's reports, as was common for Shire Secretaries everywhere, provided the gloss that described Council's balance sheet, municipal works, service provision, industrial issues and community activity. While this report would be no different in intent and content, next Monday's agenda carried an item of interest to all the good folk of Bowater. The proposed site for the Shire's new landfill to accommodate the growing mountain of refuse accumulated weekly by the burgeoning throw-away society, had stirred ripples of debate among the locals. The replacement of the old, exhausted waste tip would require some acute social and political engineering and the massaging of vested self-interest. Conflict of interest was writ large over this agenda item, innocuously titled, 'Landfill Options'. The Shire Engineer's preferred option of the two up for consideration was a natural depression in a large tract of land on the southern outskirts of town. He dismissed as a less viable option, a site to the east of the river and nearer to the homes of those mired in misfortune, the impotent and the disenfranchised. The Engineer would argue that the proposed proximity to the river presented the risk of seepage and the tainting of the river upstream of the town centre. All compounded by the fact that the town drew its water from the treatment plant that would be adjacent to the new tip should this, against the Engineer's wishes, be the preferred site for a landfill. Devereau instinctively knew that objective analysis and reasoned argument would wilt under an avalanche of privilege and hypocrisy. For the Engineer's preferred site abutted parcels of land held by two of Council's most influential, powerful and vociferous members. Councillors, who, together with their allies and force of will, would exalt the preservation of mutual interest and the protection of personal domain. All cloaked in subterfuge and shrouded in municipal legitimacy under the banner of the common good. Devereau ruminated on the outcome, but intuitively knew the debate would be brief, riddled with obfuscation and self-justification. Depending on how Councillor Freeman voted, the Engineer would be rolled with very little rancour and a healthy majority of at least 7 to 2. Privately, Devereau supported his Engineer's considered assessment, but political instinct and the god of self-preservation warned him against risking his municipal longevity by opposing a foregone conclusion. Consequently, his report left the issue open with his only advice being for the careful consideration of both options.

Devereau, having completed his report and given it to Millie, his secretary, for typing, sat gazing out at a community going about its business. A melancholy settled over his being as he reflected on his reluctance to take a stand on the landfill matter and his failure to give Council the qualitative advice for which he was employed. He reconciled his misgiving with the trappings of office, the needs of his family and survival in the incestuous harem that was municipal politics. Just three months before, the *Bowater Bugle*, founded in 1931, had paid a glowing tribute to the recently arrived Shire Secretary with the banner headline,

'*William Devereau: Bowater's New Go Getter*'. The story told of Devereau's municipal career and how he was plucked from the City of Northcote where he earned a reputation as a professional with a steely resolve to get things done. As Deputy Manager of the Planning Department, he had overseen the commercial, social and cultural development of its post-war suburbs. These once stagnant suburbs had been tenderly massaged into vibrant, prosperous hubs. *The Bugle*, effusive in its canonisation of Devereau, chided the community to get behind his endeavours to make the town a thriving centre that lived up to its motto of, '*Prosperity through Toil*'. To become a rural beacon that lights the fires of harmony, Christian charity and hard work eulogised the *Bugle* from its noble pulpit.

William Deavereau had left school at fifteen and, in late 1929, began work as an assistant in the dispatch office of the Small Arms Ammunition Factory (No.1) in Footscray. He was indeed very fortunate, as his uncle, who was close to one of the factory's supervisors, managed to get him work at the factory. The economic contagion that was the Wall Street crash had yet to cascade Australia into depression and the young Devereau, through family connection, had managed to find secure employment in a government ordinance factory. A ringing endorsement of one of his father's favourite maxims, 'It's not what you are son, but who you know. That is the key to success in this world. Just you remember it.' By 1939 he had met, fallen in love and married Alice White. At which time he had risen through the ranks to become chief clerical officer in charge of dispatch. The advent of World War 2 saw the factory continue its operations and as his was deemed a reserved occupation, he, choosing not to seek an exemption, didn't enlist and head off to the battlefields of Europe. A circumstance, that to this day brings on pangs of guilt whenever he attends Remembrance Day services, or in his dealings with the widows of fallen soldiers. With war's end, Footscray's small arms manufacturing factory closed its doors for good, whereupon Devereau found himself employed as a clerk with the City of Northcote's Rates Department. Peter, his only child was born in 1942, and he was greatly relieved to have turned up a job with Northcote, which became a city in 1914. He studied accounting and transport with RMIT at nights and worked diligently to forge a career in local government. When the Bowater Shire position became vacant, he applied. While not expecting to win the role of Shire Secretary, he was determined to expand his work experience and fashion a good life for he and his family. Little did he know that he came highly recommended for the position by the Town Clerk, who saw Devereau as a threat to his job. He was effusive in his praise when Cyril Dixon contacted him seeking comment on Devereau's qualities, skills and work ethic. Sold on Devereau, Cyril Dixon was determined that he was the man to take on the Shire Secretary's role at Bowater.

Devereau, a waggish smile evoking the memory of his welcome, tidied his desk and with a mental shrug of resigned compliance, farewelled his staff and strolled from his office.

He was glad the day was done, but found only trepidation as the gremlins of his mind conjured up portents of misgiving and the devil of controversy as thoughts of next week's Council meeting invaded his sensitivities.

Waiting at the opened front door was the welcoming embrace of a wife who, by force of habit, asked how his day had panned out. 'Okay, I guess,' came his practised response. As has been his want over the last 16 years, work stopped at his front door, where home began. On seeing Peter, he asked, too by force of habit, how his day had been.

'Some older boys pushed Aadje around a bit after school and our art and music teachers have left and won't be coming back any more,' he added.

'That's no good. Do you know why they've gone?' his father asked.

'Nup,' was the response from Peter who promptly disappeared into the sanctity of his room.

'That's an unusual state of affairs,' Devereau mused to no one in particular.

'Very strange indeed,' he muttered.

CHAPTER FOUR

Deliverance

Breakfast in the Devereau household followed a familiar ritual. Peter and his father sat at the laminex table, perched on chromium legged dining chairs, resplendent in cracked beige vinyl and accents of red piping. Peter's crutches, propped against the end of the square dining table, with its rounded corners protected by aluminium strips, was one of the many items of clutter his mother negotiated each morning. Alice Devereau, turbaned auburn hair, full length apron and pink slippers, distributed the cereal and toast with practised dexterity and familiarity. Devereau's Council papers, neatly piled, ruled one end of the table, while the only vacant chair was the domain of the slippered matriarch.

'You'd better hurry, you two, or you'll be late,' smiled Alice Devereau. Getting them off to work and school was a mission she inherited on marriage and motherhood all those many years ago.

Peter, with satchel on back and callipers locked, snatched his supports from table's end and made his way, followed by his father, out the front door. As normal his mission was to meet up with Aadje at Curlin's Bridge. From there the two friends ambled their way to school. As was their bent, they made haste slowly so as to arrive as classes start to avoid the barbs of Aadje's older, stronger and menacing protagonists. Standing on a grassy knoll, casting a casual eye over the backdrop, they absorbed the sloping, corroded banks of a river stroked by gums, willows and gently swaying reeds on its flight north. Water birds played with the insects and broke the calm with a cacophony of whistles, whoops and shrieks. Aadje of short and gangly frame, idly threw clods of dirt into the beckoning river and with each concentric circle, ever widening, looked up at Curlin's Bridge.

'I'm gonna dive off there in summer,' Aadje affirmed, stabbing a determined finger in the direction of the bridge.

'Why would you wanna do that? It's too high, you'll kill yourself,' censured Peter.

'All the kids do it and I'm gonna show 'em I'm as good as they are. Then they'll stop pickin' on me,' rejoined Aadje, with a tone of finality that once more stirred mild concern somewhere deep in Peter's core.

'Still,' thought Peter. 'It won't happen. It is just wishful thinking and Aadje is only saying it 'cause it makes him feel good.'

Leaving the tranquillity and comfort of the river's embrace, the two made their way to school, a path tracked and wracked with familiarity and resignation. As was feared, Blackie, like a praying mantis gorging on Aadje's carcass of vulnerability, met them with preordained sinister intent and a verbal assault that referenced Aadje's parentage, stature and status. Out of school Aadje and Peter found solace in their own company. When left to the freedom of their own devices, they could escape the travesties of persecution and the travails of torment by wandering aimlessly through the sights and sounds of Bowater's majestic past and present.

Down by the Empire Hotel and out through the sale-yards, was the sandy enclave of the local swimming hole. Transplanted palms contradicted the natural vegetation of gums and willows and gave an ambience, even in winter, of a summer yet to come. Peter and Aadje would sit and talk of all things, of their shadowed present and optimism for the future. Aadje dreamed of being a truck driver where, in splendid isolation, he would be left alone to be himself. For Peter, his future ended at his callipered legs and despaired of ever joining the navy. The highlight of their surreptitious meandering was to steal looks through the dust stained windows of the local funeral home. A wooden shed, serving as the mortuary and embalming room, provided Aadje and Peter with many a secret story to tell. *A.K. Bromwich, Funeral Director,* announced a faded shingle at its front entrance to the shed that defined the macabre goings-on inside this ramshackle building. Just fifty yards from the river bank and shaded by ever present gums, it carried a stainless-steel embalming table, a marble slab discoloured by time and the rust-like hues of dried blood, a concrete floor of the same dappled colours and lining the wall, was a seven foot by three foot freezer. The boys learned much of the frailty of the dead in their clandestine observation of the embalmer at work and talked long of their experiences and the wonder of mortality.

It was here that they saw Jericho Jack laid out in all his gruesome and not so former glory. Jack, in his late sixties, was a drover of some renown in the district and regularly herded cattle and sheep through the outskirts of town. His undoing came with his habit of sleeping under his wagon in the company of his tethered kelpies. Having taken leave of this mortal coil, sometime during the night, when he was visited by cardiac arrest, it was nearly a week before what was left of Jericho Jack was found. His tethered companions, suffering the worst of starvation, chose the tough and wizened flesh of their master as their dawn of salvation. The sight that confronted Sgt. O'Reilly when called to the scene convulsed him with nausea. Taking a gun from the boot of his car, he dispatched the three dogs to perfidy and scrambled off to get the town's undertaker to take care of business. Jericho Jack, so named because, as a drover, he had claimed to have seen the Promised Land. While the locals suspected a surfeit of whisky and hallucination as the prime motivation for his pilgrimage to Mecca, the name, however, stuck. A transient drover rounded up Jericho's straying sheep and Jericho Jack was no more. Interned in an unmarked grave, his passing was to become, over time, the stuff of fable and fantasy. Of particular amusement for the two boys was the undertaker keeping the purity of his fresh catch of Murray Cod and red-fin in the bowels of the very freezer that was the temporary resting place of all cadavers enjoying the last of their temporal being. The fish lay silent, keeping life's flotsam company in a dance stilled by death and decomposition. Peter's mother could never fathom his sudden and unexpected aversion to fish of any sort. He could never come clean of course. For to do so, would be a betrayal of friendship and conspire against secrecy and the thrill of adolescence.

Saturdays and football had seen Aadje show Peter the perfect place to sneak across the river and into Kendall's Reserve without paying for the privilege. Peter, while struggling across the broad trunk of a tree fallen as a bridge over the watery barricade downstream, managed it with daring and manipulative dexterity. With Aadje to hold his crutches, Peter straddled his bridge of delinquency and shimmied himself across on his nether regions. The tell-tale scuffs on his pants being the only evidence of a crime motivated by audacity and Aadje's shortage of money. Committee men, awake to the subterfuge, trolled the river bank with the expectation that they could collar any interlopers by the neck and hand them over to Sgt. O'Reilly for the dispensing of his rough take on justice. Their best intentions, however, were easily thwarted by laying low among the grasses carpeting the river bank and awaiting the inevitable onset of boredom and the game's ebb and flow to drive them back to the Committee Rooms. Senior games were broadcast on Radio CCV and called by a stalwart of the local airwaves, Dick Craddock. Craddock's signature dub was, *'I'll call the board,'* followed by the score. Blackie and his cronies, having already played for the Bowater Thirds, would congregate at the bottom of the wooden broadcast box and, in unison, yell out, 'here boardy, boardy,' each time Craddock let loose his customary rallying cry of, 'I'll call the board.' Blackie and his choir of locusts would disperse on first sight of Sgt. O'Reilly heading in their direction. Overweight from too long a soft billet and red faced from exertion, they were long gone by the time the long arm of the law had arrived. It was but a game to Blackie and he exploited every opportunity to repeat the exercise. Whenever the good Sergeant drifted to the other side of the ground, the ever-vigilant Blackie and his friends would return to populate the sizable vacuum once filled by Sgt. O'Reilly's ample, if breathless, proportions. From a safe distance, Aadje and Peter enjoyed Blackie's little exercise in trouble making and secretly wished they could join in. A spiritual enthusiasm tempered by Peter's lack of pace which meant that even a ponderous Sgt. O'Reilly would be able to run him down.

The boys often visited the local Chinese market gardener, Chen Kwong, who had four acres of land on the river bank some one hundred yards upstream from the town's weir. Seventy-year-old Chen was the only child of Oriental parents. They were the remnants of the influx of Chinese who had earlier invaded the diggings in search of alluvial gold and its bounty. When the gold and the promise of riches ran out, they settled in Bowater and crafted a vegetable garden by the river and hawked vegetables around the fledgling settlement and, later, to Sergio Sgro's Fruit & Vegetable Emporium.

While Chen inherited the market garden on the passing of his parents, he never managed to find a bride. He, like the two friends, found no welcoming mat in Bowater and was an isolate who, except when hawking his wares, kept very much to himself. His market garden became both his companion and his salvation. He enjoyed the boys' company and, in his solid English, regaled them with his father's stories, tall and true from the glory days of the gold rush. An era where the Chinese were vilified, assaulted and cursed as opium fuelled, heathen savages taking jobs, women and wealth. Realising little had changed since the days of his father, Chen Kwong found it more comforting and safer to beat a hasty retreat into the sanctity of his own isolation. The two boys enlightened and enlivened Chen and he looked forward to their occasional forays into his cloistered province where Aadje would ravenously devour any vegetable he deemed worthy of eating. It was on these occasions, Aadje was able to take some bounteous gifts of vegetables home to his mother who sometimes had fresh produce for the table, thanks to the largesse and kindness of a Chinese market gardener, ostracised by a world to which he owed nothing.

The boys' itinerant travels took them past the ornate portals of the Strand Theatre, where Peter's mother and father sometimes took him to see the feature film of the day. A privilege never afforded Aadje whose mother supplemented her widow's pension by doing other people's washing and cleaning. Simply, she could not afford Aadje the luxury. They also came across swagmen, drabbed out in worn boots, torn dungarees, tattered shirt and a jacket adorned with their swag slung across weary shoulders and their billy, burned black, hanging from the rope that masqueraded as a belt. These were the sundowners. Their faces lined with years of frugality and sun, wind and rain. The broad brimmed hat, shielding a bearded, unkempt visage that bespoke of a past riddled with disaster, despair and isolation. Of an existence beset with failure and lonely resignation. Whenever a swaggie knocked on the door of the Devereau household, Alice would warily give the unfortunate a jam sandwich and send him on his way. A charity sought at a number of likely residences as they wended their way out of Bowater in search of another town and a place to rest a weary head. Sgt. O'Reilly gave a good impression of removing the welcome from the Bowater mat for any homeless undesirable who blew through. But his Irish heart just wasn't in it and conspired to make himself scarce at the most strategic of times. A circumstance not lost on the well-endowed, the barons of business and the good burghers of Bowater. For them, the shiftless and the ungodly are blights on the good name of the town, and must be turned away. The fortress of superiority shall not be breached. Personal domain and material space are sacrosanct and must not be sullied. They demanded protection. It is the constabulary's job to keep Bowater safe from the drift-wood that the winds of ill-will blow through. For the residents inhabiting the enclave of privilege, Sgt. O'Reilly was lacking and the seeds of discontent took sprout in the fertile soil cultivated by the disaffected and the affluent.

Peter had on occasion visited Aadje's house and saw first-hand the difficulties weighing heavily on what was left of the Kuiper family. The two-bedroom cottage had fallen into disrepair since his father's death. While the garden demonstrated care and attention, the pickets, like stained and broken teeth, were coming adrift from the front fence. Modest surrounds belayed Anki Kuiper's unrequited love for her son and the wrenching grief at the loss of her daughter and husband. Photographs on the cracked mantelpiece showed Geert Kuiper to be a thin, but agile looking man with wispy blond hair and matching goatee beard. His hollow cheeks, prominent white teeth and thin lips framed a smile that spoke of much ambition. Aadje's little sister by photograph, was a mirror image of her mother. Brown hair, wide eyes and high cheekbones sang of a daughter whose heritage was beyond question. Aadje helped his mother when he could. Collecting washing and returning it clean and pressed was his sacrifice to the laws of status and his station in life. No matter how ungainly, Peter, sympathy abounding, was always glad to get home after one of his visits to Aadje's place. His California bungalow by comparison, was well kept, inviting and a refuge from the ravages of a world destined to mock his frailty. His mother had the Bakelite radio tuned to Radio CCV by ritual, where the musical strains of 1955 filtered throughout the Devereau household. Louis Armstrong's, *Blueberry Hill* and Tony Bennett's, *Stranger in Paradise*, in all its irony, would meander down the passage and find their way onto the front verandah. From there they rhapsodically commingled with the songs of birds and the rustle of trees. For Peter, the lilting melody of Burl Ives letting loose with, *Lavender Blue,* joined with all the others to present a musical barricade against the vagaries of life in a small country town. He was home and he was comforted in its welcoming warmth. A warmth only shattered by the unannounced visit by the Radio Inspector checking that all who dared possess a radio were licenced to operate the dials of civilisation. With seemingly more investigative powers than Sgt. O'Reilly, they could, with unfettered authority and legislative sanction, knock on any door and demand to see the licence as proof of legality. The Devereau's were financially positioned to renew their licence, while the battlers, like the Kuiper's, were hit with the injustice that poverty visits, of intimidation and fines disproportionate to the offence. Aadje's mother dispensed with the comfort of her prized radio following a visit by an inspector, wherein she displayed extreme criminality by hiding the family radio under a bed and covering it with ladies' unmentionables. Anxiety and fear beset the poor woman who conformed to the mores of contemporary society by jettisoning her only comfort to the confines of the local landfill.

CHAPTER FIVE

Trysts & Turns

Bill Devereau, snatching up his Council papers into his briefcase, followed his son out the front door and with a casual, 'See ya,' to his wife began the half mile trek through town to his office in the Council Chambers. When he arrived, his secretary and the Shire's clerical officer were already in place and preparing themselves for the day ahead. With the standard courtesy of chorused, 'Good Mornings,' Devereau ensconced himself behind his desk and busied himself with the subtleties of local government. Millie had typed his report for Monday's Council meeting and had neatly positioned it in his '*in-tray*' and awaited his editing and final approval. Having determined that the deteriorating road surface in Kriall Street could wait, he reflectively thumbed through the sheath of papers to his, as yet unread, Council report. As he absorbed the words he had scripted, his mind jangled with thoughts of the coming Council meeting and the potential for acrimonious, if one-sided, debate and an outcome likely to be steeped in injustice and jaundiced by vested interest. Besides the Shire Secretary, the Engineer and the Health Inspector represented the executive arm of municipal affairs and spent their waking hours in grand appeasement of the competing forces of finance, staffing, service provision and public works. Each of the three officers, dependant on portfolio, were responsible for revenue and expenditure and, on a monthly basis, were required to report and justify all for Council approval. Matters of rates, sanitation, debt-servicing, Council properties, roads and bridges were generally rubber stamped in a harmonious expression of entitled self-preservation. Monday's meeting, though, would see the landfill debate flare and this, in the brewing, had filled Devereau with the spectre of alarm and contrition. Devereau's report, in its detail, related the options open to Council, but was consciously silent when it came to his preference for the location of the new landfill. Contrary to the Engineer's Council report, Devereau offered no direction on the matter, and by leaving the outcome to the elected burghers he could distance himself from the conundrum, cleanse himself of guilt, protect his Council support base and salve his conscience. Having been with the Shire of Bowater a mere three months, he had no stomach for jeopardising his longevity by antagonising the elected councillors whose status enriched tentacles ruled the town. So what if there was some collateral damage to justice, logic and town amenity. Bowater and its good citizens would move on and his Engineer would survive to fight another day.

Having perused the agenda and the reports of his officers,

he called Millie and instructed that the papers be distributed. As the forty-five-year -old Millie Duggan, sartorial in blue jacket, matching skirt and high heels, diligently shuffled the papers and left the room, his office door burst open and, framed in a halo of light and anxiety, stood the Shire President.

'I need to see you. It's urgent. We've got a problem,' demanded Cr Dixon in a tone stressed by the weight of municipal responsibility. Devereau, somewhat taken aback, raised his eyebrows and gazed at the apparition filling his office doorway.

'I know about Kriall Street,' was all that lamely escaped his open mouth. Cr Dixon, as usual, sockless and sporting his crumpled three-piece suit, closed the door, threw his hat onto Devereau's conference table and conspiratorially pulled up a seat close to Devereau's desk. After a none too subtle scan of the room to ensure the primacy of privacy, his darting eyes met Devereau's, and, in a voice not much above a whisper, recited the, 'we've got a problem,' that heralded his colourful entrance to Devereau's office.

'What's the problem, Councillor?' asked his Shire Secretary, fearing the worst.

'You would have heard about the two teachers from the school who were shovelled out of town over the holidays. Did you hear anything?' queried the Shire President.

'Only that my son told me that two teachers had left the school,' Devereau responded, unsure of the significance.

'Well, the problem is that two of our long-standing Councillors are involved and it's got to be hushed up and buried to protect the good name of Bowater. We mustn't have a scandal. It wouldn't look too good,' Cr Dixon rasped, surging with barely disguised shame, tinged with a hint of smug superiority.

In a voice addled with confusion and intrigue, Devereau asked the Shire President to explain. In the telling, it appears that two buxom, if not wholesome teachers, complemented their scanty incomes by turning tricks after class and at night in a little flat that doubled as a clandestine house of ill-repute. Its clientele, as was fashionable for the time, were drawn from the social milieu best described as the elite. Customers, under cover of darkness, would squirrel in for some discrete pleasures of the night. Two regulars of rank and social standing just happened to be the Deputy Shire President and a councillor endowed with reputation and respect as reward for his years of service to the citizens of Bowater. Three weeks ago, when the constabulary finally, through the drift of gossip, rumour and innuendo, wakened to the teachers' extra-curricular activity and visited the flat, they found, besides the two councillors, the local bank manager. Lamed by shame and fear, the councillors and bank manager were unceremoniously sent home by Sgt. O'Reilly and his constable to await the outcome of his investigation. Devereau, smiling inwardly, paid silent tribute to the enterprise of the teachers and their capacity for turning a quid asked, 'What happened then?' He was warming to the conspiracy and to the discomfort of others that only innocence can bring. Cr Dixon continued without pause and described the sordid episode in detail. For to lay charges, would have sullied reputations and fractured the peace and good order of Bowater. So in the interests of expediency and, with ranks closed around the good name of the privileged, no charges were laid. In the meantime, the two attractive young teachers were, with uncommon haste, spirited back to the anonymity of the big smoke. From whence the ripples of scandal, muted by conspiracy, silence, intrigue and subterfuge, washed over the town and saved it from spiralling into a psychosis of burned reputations and cynical mockery. By closing the book on the squalid affair, Sgt. O'Reilly would be able to go about his duties imbued and emboldened by the sublime and lordly comfort that comes with the moral high ground, and of an elite beholding to his silence. The golden chalice of redemption, salvation and saved marriages was once more in the vestry of the righteous. Their humiliation was but quarantined between the cover up and the denial and all would again be well with Bowater. The lofty perch of the miscreant and the venerated was once more safe from calamitous misfortune. Having finished his dissertation, Cr Dixon asked, more in expectation than revelation, 'what should we do?'

'Nothing. I wouldn't worry about it,' was Devereau's nonchalant retort. Supressing a tingling excitement and hiding a somewhat conceited smile that threatened to curl at his lips, Devereau simply said, 'tell Cr Owen and Cr McNichol to lay low. The mill that grinds the rumour will eventually stall. In the meantime, simple denial and scoff will continue to massage indifference, confuse and deflect. While, the town will be ripe with all sorts of lurid and tainted tales, only a few will know all the detail. For the majority of good folk, the story will be nothing but pub talk. A fallacious rumour spread by those with an axe to grind and reputations to sully. If everybody keeps their mouth shut and goes to ground, it will, like everything else, pass into figment and fable. It will be our little secret, won't it?' theorised Devereau, while mentally filing his version of folklore in the darkened recess of his mind reserved for possible future use. Filed, but not to be forgotten, the Shire President's sordid tale of intrigue would secure a prime berth, in what Devereau amusingly described as his leverage file.

'I hope you're right,' lamented Cr Dixon, with an air of reservation and resignation. With that, the Shire President slid back his chair and, with a swoop that would do a peregrine falcon proud, snatched up his hat and whereupon, four strides later, he exited Devereau's office without fanfare. Left alone and in silence, Devereau, savouring the glory of revelation and conspiracy, smiled with fleeting admiration at the financial guile of the teachers and shook his head with dismay at the compromising stupidity of Bowater's finest. It was a folly forged in arrogance, tempered with delusions of grandeur and it saw two councillors and a bank manager caught in a clandestine web of their own making. For them, status corroded normal compliance with the social mores and strictures of a community founded on Christian values and morality. It gave them the illusion of the untouchable and, in the natural order of things, a cut above the very citizens they deem to serve.

The Council agenda was, barring the landfill issue, bathed in the normalcy of municipal general business. Perennials such as road works, footpaths, parks and gardens, sanitation, revenue and industrial matters were all listed for discussion. It is to these that Devereau spent the afternoon preparing for the regular questions from councillors as each issue related to their individual ridings. Each councillor represented one of the Shire's nine ridings, some rural, some residential, and were elected for a three-year term. Of the nine councillors, Dixon, Owen, Curlin and McGregor had served multiple terms and as the power elite, formed a cohort of landed gentry, that, when yoked to Crs Ferguson and McNichol from the field of business and commerce, established a formidable voting bloc. Their unbridled electoral success, predetermined by a heady mix of sinecure, wealth, privilege, religion and community networks, meant that they were electorally unassailable and beyond challenge from citizens of lesser rank or file. They, in substance and action, formed a potent factional alliance cemented by the ties of mutual benefit, conservative social values and arrogance. They of the messiah complex, were in belief and deed, born to rule, and their individual success was proof positive of their exalted status and capacity to lead. A circumstance not lost on the citizenry who, by force and necessity, must show deference by genuflecting before the altar of those who know best. A fellow traveller and, when it suited, an honorary member of the alliance was Cr Adrian Freeman. His elevation to the Shire of Bowater owed much to his religious proclivity and the support of the twenty three percent of Bowater's population who are followers of the Catholic faith. Cr Freeman was neither wealthy, nor particularly privileged. Having arrived in Bowater prior to war's end, when he was fortuitously able to liberate Shen Cheung's Chinese laundry when he was found unexpectedly deceased behind the front counter of his shop. Cr Freeman took the strictures of laity in his stride, promoting and defending the faith at every opportunity. He regaled against the evils of communism and was a strident advocate of state aid. His politics of reaction and membership of the DLP made him a natural ally, but not a member, of the conservative, protestant power elite. He praised his God for delivering Victoria from the left wing, communist inspired, Cain Labour Government and delivering the right-thinking Henry Bolte as Victoria's new Liberal Premier.

'Thing's will be better for the bush now that Cain's gone,' he would tell anybody with an ear to listen. Cr Freeman dressed his anti-communism in the vestments of a zealot, fervently pressed by a chorus of Cardinals, Bishops, Archbishops and the vocal Catholic laity. A secular shield, ordained in the sanctity of the church, proclaimed from the pulpit and promulgated through the gospel according to B.A. Santamaria and his Catholic Social Studies Movement. As a Catholic, Adrian Freeman took his lay apostolic duties as a summons from his God to rid the world of the communist menace and propagate the faith among the heathen and the lapsed. Promote and defend was the holy credos of a mind steeped in conspiracy and paranoia. Cr Freeman wore his messianic robes as a badge of honour and used them as a club to smite his enemies, both real and imagined. The two remaining councillors, Hughie Keegan and Samuel Clark, shunned by the others, formed a duumvirate whose genesis owed more to necessity than to the confluence of social and political values. Voting as a bloc of two at least gave mutual support in debates. They were just an echo in defence of the dispossessed and disaffected. A duet welded in the belief that the less fortunate, the mute and the cowed should have a voice in municipal affairs. Keegan, at fifty-two, a former shearer, tiring of the itinerant life, wet sheep and disgruntled pastoralists, abandoned the industry to set up shop as a contract fencer, come handyman. Keegan, well read and articulate, was prone to grand oratory sweetly burnished with a mix of eloquence and arrogance. A circumstance that saw him branded as batting above his station by his council opponents. It is rumoured Keegan is a closet member of the Australian Labor Party and, as is the stuff of gossip, it is believed that this innuendo, whispered behind closed doors and pursed lips, coloured a swag of Bowater East ratepayers and prompted them to exact sweet revenge on the elite and elect him to council. Clark, a lineman with the State Electricity Commission, a home owner, domiciled in Bowater, was elected on the basis of his youthful good looks, energy and gift of the gab. Bowater's aging belles fell for his ego-stroking charm and provided the stimulus to his narrow election victory. The ruling clique, in stunned disbelief, were consumed with a revenge fuelled by angst, discomfort and foreboding. For them, the erosion of municipal control was but the Trojan horse of the inferior breaching the battlements of good governance. It left them as a battalion under siege and fostered ever greater resolve to close ranks and, phalanx like, repel democracy's vandals. In cynical conspiracy, they vowed to protect the tenets of wealth and privilege through vitriol, denigration and weight of numbers at every opportunity.

'It is the thin edge of the wedge. They know nothing about municipal affairs and the needs of Bowater,' cried a despairing Dixon. For a horrified Freeman, it was, simply, a matter to the barricades for all. The surprise election of Clark and Keegan was the consequence of commitment and diligence as they assiduously worked the streets and promoted themselves and their anti-establishment credentials far and wide. Their constituents silently railed against the born to rule mantra of the conservative candidates and voted, albeit secretly, with their feet. Of course, Clark's charm offensive did little harm to his electoral stocks. With satisfaction writ large on their collective conscious, the locals saw the cloistered sanctity of the power brokers invaded with the elevation of Keegan and Clark to the hallowed portals of local government. It was an incursion with much to laud, and to expect.

During his time as Shire Secretary, Devereau had witnessed a preponderance of matters under discussion resolved with the unanimous support of all councillors. On the other hand, contentious issues were, where sectional interests came to play, determined by the overwhelming numbers owned by the conservative alliance and reflected the political structure of the chamber. In these circumstances, votes of seven to two were common, while six to three was a rarity. With the numbers only flexing when Cr Freeman, jettisoning his honorary membership of the ruling clique and bucking his innate opposition to most of the views espoused by the two interloping agitators, voted with them. Monday night's debate on the landfill site, he predicted, would be a short-lived flurry of verbosity and acrimony, followed by a vote of 7 to 2 in favour of developing the site in Bowater East. Devereau's quiet introspection was disturbed by the imperious figure of Cr Freeman appearing as if by magic in front of his desk. Somewhat startled, Devereau leaned back in his chair and, eyeing Freeman with his ubiquitous hat cocked awkwardly on his head, awaited him to say his piece.

'You know about the depot workers threatenin' to strike if they don't get more money, don't you?' groaned Freeman, stabbing a bony finger at Devereau for emphasis.

'The Engineer and I have discussed it. But we're just waiting to see how the basic wage case due before the Arbitration Commission works out. The depot blokes might get their pay rise through Federal determination and avoid having to deal with us. They're upset that automatic indexation for basic pay adjustments was dropped a couple of years ago,' explained Devereau, barely disguising the frustration in his voice.

'I hear Alby Trotter is the one stirring up the blokes

and spoiling for a fight. He's a member of the Municipal Employees' Union and a communist you know. They cause problems, these commies and get everyone fired up. They have a strike so they can undermine good order and take over. You've only got to have a look at what the maritime and shearers' unions have done. They stir up trouble whenever they want, just to bring the country to its knees,' lectured Freeman. Devereau, his faced creased with incredulity, looked up at the councillor and, in a voice calm with reason, pointed out that Alby Trotter was one of the municipal garbage collectors who had a wife and four kids to feed. Agitating for more money could either make him a good father or, indeed, a greedy trouble maker, but it doesn't make him a communist or communist sympathiser.

'The MEU haven't been too problematic in recent times either. Try living on their wage councillor, before you judge them or their motives,' finished Devereau.

'I think you're wrong there, Bill. The depot's full of 'em and you need to clean them out before they destroy all that we've built and stand for. Mark my words, this pay thing is just the start. We got rid of Cain because him and his mates were commie fellow travellers and if you don't do something about Alby Trotter and the others, they'll ruin us,' were Freeman's parting words as he turned on his heel and disappeared into the foyer where he vaporised from view.

With a sigh, Devereau made his way from behind his desk to close his office door. Cr Freeman, either by design or accident never deemed it a courtesy to close Devereau's door on leaving his office. An annoyance not lost on Devereau who, from the first time they met, had trouble warming to a councillor whose reactionary rendering of municipal rule was crowned in conspiracy and singed with paranoia. Cr Freeman left Devereau with the chill of despair and the realisation of a municipality governed by phobia. With a slow shake of his head, Devereau called to Millie and let her know he was heading upstairs to talk with Andy. Shire Engineer, Andrew Dawson's office was on the second floor of the Council building and negotiated by a wide flight of stairs, worn over time by the feet of the fit, the resilient and the aggrieved. Following a cursory knock on the door marked 'Engineer', Devereau sidled in and perched himself at Andy's paper laden desk.

'G'day Bill. What's up?' was his short welcome.

'I've just had a visit, more a deputation of one, complaining about the communist trouble makers at the depot,' related Devereau.

'Let me guess. Cr Freeman,' was the Engineer's mocking response.

'Yeah! You nailed it Andy. Can you give me another update?'

'Bill, it's like I said. The boys want a pay rise, which to my mind is a reasonable proposition in this day and age. Cr Freeman is stirring up problems that aren't there by overdramatising the whole issue. I've spoken to the blokes and while they are pretty adamant, they want Council to show some good will and do the right thing, they are prepared to wait, along with their union, until the Arbitration case is finished. This gives us all a bit of breathing space,' Dawson reported.

'You think you can handle it in-house Andy?'

'Yeah, I think so. The other councillors don't seem too fussed over the issue,' came the Engineer's relaxed, if not over optimistic response.

'What is it with Cr Freeman? I can cope with the others. I understand where they're coming from. But Freeman takes reasoned argument as proof of conspiracy everywhere,' muttered Devereau, making more of a statement than asking a question.

'Look Bill, I'm of the same faith as Freeman and I attend the same Sunday mass as he does. Each Sunday, the priest, as part of his sermon, will read a lengthy epistle from the Archbishop decrying the evils of communists and their fellow travellers, eulogising over the primacy of Catholicism and beseeching all to go forth and promulgate the faith. Stressing the duty of the laity to serve God, the church and, through Catholic Action, confront the evil beset with destroying the Christian ethos held so dear by the true believers. Cr Freeman is convinced, by some clever fear mongering, that the church and all who sail in her are under siege from a contagion so vast that recourse to God alone will not save its soul. This is the ethereal realm that Freeman and many others inhabit. A paranoia that strips contemporary affairs of reasoned analysis and denies the church and its parishioners the spiritual benefit of open discourse and the battlefield of ideas,' was Dawson's enlightened offering. 'Cr Freeman carries his own version of the *Malleus Maleficarum* in his back pocket. You've got to understand, for the Freeman's of the world there is no gap between gospel and culture. They are but one in the same thing.'

'Jesus Andy. I had no idea,' said a spiritually confused Devereau, completely lost on this Malleus thing.

'That makes you and half my brethren. Well Bill, this is not the same parish I served as an altar boy all those years ago. I don't like where the church is heading. The clandestine infiltration of unions, political parties and community organisations, all with the avowed aim of directing values and taking control is not, to my way of thinking, in the best interests of the church. When such guerrilla activities enjoy the financial support of the hierarchy it can only create angst among Christians of all faiths and set the church up for ridicule and decline. I would appreciate keeping our little discussion to yourself. I don't wish to become a leper in my own church,' extolled the Engineer, as he trolled for secrecy.

'Not a worry. I won't breathe a word. This goes some way to explaining why Evatt went after the Industrial Groups that caused the ALP to split this year,' conspired Devereau, dispatching his new-found oath of silence to his leverage file.

'You have it in one,' were Andy's parting words, as Devereau left the Engineer's lofty perch to make his way back to the comfort of his own office and the mantle of his authority.

Following the revelations of the past week, bordello's and communist conspiracies notwithstanding, and the flurry of activity that comes with local government, the scheduled

Council meeting rolled around quickly. Monday afternoon found Devereau and Millie busy in preparation for that night's meeting only three hours hence. As was tradition, born of the need for sustenance, Council was preceded by a light repast at six o'clock before councillors and officers assembled for the formal meeting at seven. Liturgically, proclaimed by a stroke of the ornate grandfather clock sequestered behind the Shire President's presiding chair. Either side of the President sat the Shire Secretary to his right, with the Engineer and Health Inspector occupying seats to his left. Arraigned before him, in a horseshoe of high-backed chairs, lustrous in green leather, were the elected councillors. The mahogany Council table, with its green leather inserts, sported copies of minutes from the last meeting and note paper adorned with the Council crest, together with a sharpened pencil should municipal fervour grip them with the need to take notes. Such is the routine and the ritual subscribed to all Council meetings and tonight's proved to be no different in its coming together. The Shire President, bedecked in the robes of office and in the most imperious manner he could muster, opened the meeting with a welcome and a reading of the Lord's Prayer. Having pointed out the order of business as listed in the agenda before them, the Chair asked for other items of urgent business not incorporated in the agenda as distributed. The usual issues of roads, bridges, footpaths, garbage, and swaggies were raised by various riding councillors to placate the ire of disgruntled constituents and to exalt their self-image and stroke their messianic egos. Devereau was a little surprised that Cr Freeman had not listed the MEU and its wage push for discussion. He had convinced himself that Freeman would use the issue as the spoon to stir up opposition against the union and the depot workers' quest for a pay increase. By sowing the seeds of conflict in fertile soil early, germination would coincide with the heightened demands of the workers and play into Freeman's hands. Devereau could only conclude that Freeman was keeping his powder dry for a more propitious time. Council moved through its agenda with little rancour as the Kriall Street deterioration was discussed and determined to be a high priority and would be funded in the next round of estimates. Cr Keegan noted, with a smirk, that the said street was west of the river and smack in the heart of Cr Ferguson's riding. Keegan, however, recognised and accepted that the street was in need of major upgrade and supported it on that basis. Cr Owen, along with Cr McNichol, the subjects of vague rumour blowing through the town's underbelly regarding the ladies of the night, looked decidedly sheepish and uncomfortable during the debate. Their eyes spoke of apprehension lest some snide remark find its way through their chameleon hides and rot the frail flesh of secrecy and subterfuge. Crs Owen and McNichol kept as low a profile as possible this night to minimise the risk of gravitating any comments of derision, innuendo or sneer designed to embarrass or denigrate. Disconcerting to the two men was the uncertainty of who in the chamber, besides Cr Dixon, were abreast of their recent tryst and who may be simpering barbs of contented superiority behind a mask of pretence and righteousness. Devereau, as Shire Secretary, pitched for the need to replace and upgrade the Shire's current road making plant and equipment which was now eighteen years old. Council, in its entirety agreed and requested a status report and costings be prepared for next meeting with the view of referring it to estimates in October. Cr Ferguson's concerns over swaggies coming into town and frightening the children and old ladies was glossed over by determining to refer the problem back to the local constabulary for resolution. All road, footpath, sanitation and garbage matters were discussed and referred back to the responsible officer to address and report progress back to Council at its next meeting.

Debate on the site for the Shire's new landfill site, as Devereau expected, began with acrimony when Cr McGregor stood to move a motion, seconded by Cr Ferguson, that the new site be the Council owned land in Bowater East. Before the good councillor could begin his tirade of justification, Cr Keegan launched himself into the fray with a demand that Crs Curlin and Owen come clean and declare their sinister intent and not vote on the resolution. 'They don't want the tip on their doorstep and will do anything to make sure the less fortunate in Bowater East get saddled with it,' he railed.

'That's going over the top, councillor. The site of the landfill has no effect on them one way or the other.' The Shire President, irritated by the onslaught, curtly ruled Cr Keegan's objection out of order.

'Right then, let's get on with it. Move your motion councillor and make it sharp,' cajoled the President.

Cr McGregor, pudgy from being too long at the trough of culinary delight and a surfeit of amber fluid, took umbrage and launched into his calling with the zeal of a missionary.

'Thank you, Mr Shire President. It is as clear as the day that the appropriate site for the new landfill is the Council owned land at the end of Jackson's Road in Bowater East. It is a site close to the Council depot and a more convenient run for our trucks and for the residents of the Shire needing to use the tip. With careful management, I cannot foresee any problems with this location in terms of contamination. Being on the edge of town, it shouldn't present an eyesore or any health risks for the nearby residents. I know the Engineer's report mentions risks to the town's water supply because of the treatment plant's proximity to the Jackson's Road site, but I am sure that with careful monitoring, the integrity of Bowater's water supply will be protected. This issue certainly doesn't outweigh the many advantages that this site provides to the residents. The alternative site, on the southern outskirts of Bowater, is some considerable distance from the operational heart of town and adds cost in transporting waste. Its distance would be a source of frustration for our residents requiring access to the tip and the unsealed road, dare I say track, would create issues of dust in summer and be virtually impassable with mud in winter. Consequently, I commend the resolution to Council and look forward to unanimous support.'

'Thank you, Cr McGregor. Does the seconder wish to speak?'

'Not at this stage, Mr President. I will reserve my right,' was Ferguson's abrupt response, his voice resonating with his grasp of standing orders.

'Any speakers against the resolution?' the President asked. Councillor Keegan, on his feet and jabbing the bar table with a knot of stubby fingers, indicated his desire to address the matter before the chair.

'You have the floor, councillor,' instructed the Chair with a hint of undisguised frustration in his tone.

'Mr President, I find the resolution and Cr McGregor's argument in favour of Jackson's Road to be jaundiced and disingenuous in the extreme. The Shire Engineer, in his detailed report made it very clear that the risks of contamination into the Daraleet River, our water supply and the impact on the residents of Bowater East make the Jackson's Road site untenable and unsustainable as a tip site. The increased traffic, on what is a dirt track, will make life a misery for those who happen to live in this road. The site is considerably smaller than the alternative on the southern outskirts of town. Further, the southern site being some distance out of Bowater and away from the river, carries a topography that, according to our Engineer, is suited to such use and makes the southern site the most practical, cost effective alternative. As the Engineer says in his report, any risks related to seepage is nullified by soil profile and already has the value of a natural depression that can only help minimise site preparation costs. I'm sure the good councillors' sheep and crops won't suffer unduly, we have a water truck to take care of dust. My fear, Mr President, is that vested interests are attempting to highjack common sense and, by sheer weight of numbers, foist on the citizens of Bowater East a landfill the privileged don't want in their backyard. This is nothing less than councillors protecting the self-interest of their well-heeled mates on the southern end of town. Bowater deserves better, particularly when the evidence overwhelmingly supports the best location for the tip as the area of land to the south. Unfortunately, this site abuts land owned by two of our more affluent councillors and is the reason why the push is on for Jackson's Road. It would be an injustice and a trespass against reason to dump this landfill in Bowater East and must be voted down out of hand.'

'Thank you, Cr Keegan. Your grandiose assessment of your colleagues was, I'm sure, noted by those you oppose,' was the Chair's veiled warning of offence. 'Does the seconder wish to speak?'

'I do Mr Chair,' came Cr Ferguson's battle cry. 'Mr President, I take offence at Cr Keegan's remarks and find his personal attacks, laced with intimidation as they are, to be purely designed to deflect argument and logic away from what is patently clear. That being the most appropriate site for the landfill is Jackson's Road for all the reasons outlined by the mover of this resolution and contained in the Engineer's report.'

'I object Mr President,' interjected Keegan. 'The Engineer is quite clear in his recommendation that the site for the landfill should be the land to the south of the town. Cr

Ferguson is twisting the facts to suit himself,' spluttered Cr Keegan, with indignation.

'We've all read the report councillor, please sit and stay quiet. Carry on councillor.'

'Thanks Mr President. As I was saying before being rudely interrupted, the weight of objectivity and common sense leads to one inescapable conclusion. It is in the best interests of the town to site the tip in Jackson's Road, not on some dusty track miles from anywhere. Indeed, it would be a real travesty and an example of poor governance to do otherwise,' Cr Ferguson concluded.

'Before I put the motion to a vote are there any other speakers?' asked the Chair. Cr Clark rose and surveying the hounds of disinterest began to speak. 'Mr President, the Engineer's report says it all. His recommendation is considered, reasoned and, above all, realistic. To deny the efficacy of his argument for the southern site is to question Andy's credentials and credibility.'

'No one's questioning Andy's abilities councillor. So, don't try that on,' the Chair rebuked, in a tone plaited with venom.

'Nonetheless, it would be a day of shame for this Council to ignore his report in substance and opt for an inferior alternative. This resolution must be rejected and Council resolve to locate the tip to the south of the town. Besides, does Cr Ferguson know so little of his municipality that he doesn't realise that Jackson's Road is also a dusty little track, much like the one in the south he claims is unfit for the disposal of garbage,' finished Cr Cark's brief contribution to the debate.

'If that's all, I intend to put the matter to the vote. Those in favour. All those against. I declare the resolution carried.'

'Division,' was Keegan's immediate response, with a weary sigh. The Chair called for the vote again and asked his Shire Secretary to record the names of the nine councillors and how they voted for the resolution. With a majority of six to three, the motion was declared carried by the President, who promptly adjourned Council for a fifteen-minute break. Devereau was a little surprised that Cr Freeman, in abandoning his natural allies, voted against the resolution and joined his name to those of Keegan and Clark in opposing the motion to site the new landfill in Jackson's Road. Perhaps Freeman yielded to the evidence in the Engineer's report, or, maybe, he had a rush of blood in support of the disaffected and less endowed.

'The world works in mysterious ways,' reflected Devereau as he watched the councillors file from the chamber and into the little ante room where the two rival cliques would fight over tea and biscuits. As his Engineer joined him, Devereau winced when he heard the whispered and plaintiff cry from his second-in-charge. 'At least you could have said something Bill. Your silence was deafening and you left me high and dry.' In a welter of rueful discomfort, Devereau had just lost all interest in tea and biscuits and wanted the night to be over.

On reconvening, the Chair took a question from the floor on a matter relating to traffic management and the increasing number of trucks entering the town precincts to service the cannery. He took another on the need to refurbish the aging Shire Hall and, still another on the commissioning of a history of Bowater. As if on cue and preordained, all were referred to committee for consideration. 'Anything else?' the Chair asked, looking at Devereau for guidance. 'I would normally have made this item into an agenda for tonight, but given the land fill issue, I thought it best to hold it over for another time. However, I think it's appropriate to put on notice that the time is fast approaching when Council needs to consider building a new bridge over the Daraleet. Curlin's Bridge, not only is it single span, but is deteriorating at a rapid rate. Maintenance has become a time consuming, costly exercise and occasionally needs to be closed for repairs to its timber surface. I would like to put on notice, for Council's consideration, that before year's end, the Engineer and I prepare a status report on the existing bridge and design plans for a new crossing. I do warn you in advance that the cost of replacing the old bridge will be prohibitive without state government assistance. Council will need to lobby its local parliamentarians hard to open their pockets. I know the matter has been discussed previously, but continued delay in addressing the problem will only add to the long-term cost and further disadvantage travellers and ratepayers,' testified Devereau, as he ceremoniously closed his folder as a silent, if none too subtle, signal that he wished the meeting over.

'Yeah! Let's build one that those young bucks can't dive off,' commented a chorus of councillors, some of whom had done exactly that. Carrying an amused smile on the back of a pleasant memory, the Shire President declared the meeting closed at 9:45 pm, with a thank you to his Council and his officers.

Devereau was, on entering his front door, met by his wife in dressing gown and slippers.

'How was your night, dear?' she asked.

'It could have been worse,' he replied. 'All these meetings give me is more work to do and egos to stroke,' was his standard lament following Council meetings.

'Let's have some tea and call it a night,' were the soothing words of a wife who understood the power of sleep.

A Winter of Discontent

Anki Kuiper did her best to keep body and soul together. She took in as much washing and did as much cleaning as her bony hands could manage. Winter, in all its bleakness, wasn't her best season for taking in washing, but cleaning was more bountiful, if more exacting. She managed to eke out customers in competition with Freeman's laundry because she offered the convenience of pick-up and delivery. A circumstance not lost on a savvy Freeman, who was planning his own foray into the home pick-up and delivery service. Still, enough of the privileged felt sorry for the family and salved their collective consciences by off-loading their dirty linen to the battling widow of Bowater East. For them, a game of tennis took precedence over the mundane and the servitude of washing and cleaning. Mrs Kuiper, sorrowed, bitter and resigned, scrambled to give Aadje all the comfort she could muster. Love, basic meals, shelter and recycled clothes were all that she could provide. There was always a struggle to pay the bills and keep hungry creditors at bay. The house, at the end of a dusty track, was badly in need of a paint, the front window carried, like a badge of honour, a crack from top to bottom and the curtains that gave a measure of peace and blocked out the merchants of misfortune, were frayed, faded and moth eaten. The corrugated iron roof wore, like shadows in lament, signs of rust. The fly wire doors were discoloured with age and torn by the futile attempts of Aadje's Border Collie, *Towser,* to tear down the barricade that blocked access to the cool comfort and solitude of Aadje's bedroom. *Towser* mysteriously disappeared while Aadje was at school one day, believed to have been purloined by drovers as they and their sheep made their way through the district. Aadje, distraught at the disappearance of his only friend, sat for days after school at the garden gate waiting for his beloved dog to come home. A vigil, forlorn and despairing, that only ended when his mother or father called him in for tea. Where Aadje's mum would put a comforting arm around his shoulders and wipe away his tears. They shared Adje's grief at *Towser's,* disappearance, but given his deep sense of loss, they determined that a replacement would only compound his anguish and risk a repeat whenever drovers decided that they needed a sheep dog more than Aadje needed a friend.

After his father's untimely demise, Aadje did his best to help his mother. He cut the grass with his dad's old push mower and ran washing for those taking advantage of his mother's skill and good graces. Anki, seasonally adjusted, relaxed in what was left of her garden with some weeding and pruning. During summer, with dwindling supplies of tank water prioritised to the washing of other people's clothes, the garden wore its shroud of neglect. It shrivelled in the bake of a recalcitrant and merciless orb that sucked the landscape dry and parched to the core all who wore the searing mantle of the sun's summer assault. Winters in Bowater were generally mild, with rainfall topping out at about ten inches a year. Cold nights, followed by crisp mornings usually welcomed days bathed in sunshine and massaged by zephyrs wafting in from the west. Even in winter, Anki, with the help of a combustion stove, could manage to dry the clothes before Aadje needed to deliver the wares back to the owners and collect his mum's money. The house, warmed by the radiated heat from the stove, fuelled by dead wood artfully scavenged by Aadje in his many odysseys along the river bank, was spotlessly clean, but sported the ambience of a family on the edge of penury. The kitchen table, defiant in its livery of neglect and scarred by years of use was guarded by three wooden chairs of dubious heritage and quality. The lounge had seen better days, with remnants of torn fabric the legacy of *Towser's* errant paws. A sideboard crowded the room and was cluttered with sepia photographs of a long-lost daughter and much-loved husband. A family photograph held pride of place at its centre, the focus of a family split asunder by circumstances and frailty. This winter's day was, for Aadje, little different from the ones that had gone before. Aadje slung his battered satchel over his shoulders, kissed his mum goodbye and headed down the front path to meet, as had become customary over the past few months, Peter at Curlin's Bridge.

'You be good now,' his mum called as he scurried off. With a backward wave of his hand, Aadje disappeared out of sight among the gums lining the edges of the track branded, after its original inhabitant, Jackson's Road. While standing at the door, Anki spotted the greying visage of Mr Murphy leaning on her front fence.

'Hello, Mrs Kuiper. Have you heard that they're going to put a new rubbish tip at the end of our street?' barked Mr Murphy, apoplexy writ large on his stubbled face.

'No,' a frowning Anki responded.

'Yeah! We'll have trucks, traffic, dust and dirt all over us before summer ends. It's not right. This is a big Shire and couldn't they find someplace else to dump the rubbish. It'll ruin everything,' complained Mr Murphy, his Irish blood up and fissured forehead purple with rage and injustice.

'It's typical. The battlers have no say. What can we do? I take in washing and the dust will make it really hard for me,' sighed Mrs Kuiper.

'They don't care about us, or our feelin's, but I'm gonna do somethin'. You just wait and see,' Mr Murphy threatened.

'Now don't you go doin' anything silly, Mr Murphy. You'll get into strife and that wouldn't do,' was Anki's worried entreaty, a frown creasing her troubled forehead.

'I'm not gonna take this laying down. The mongrels on Council aren't gonna treat me like dirt and dump their rubbish on my door step,' were the last words he spoke. On slapping the nearest fence post and, with purpose, Murphy strode off in the direction of his humble lonely dwelling at the end of Jackson's Road. 'Oh, dear,' uttered Anki, as she turned on her heel and disappeared through the front door of her house. 'There's going to be trouble,' she thought as her mind turned to the pressing matter of Mrs Keene's washing.

Aadje met Peter, in the usual place and with a now familiar greeting. 'G'day Peter. How ya doin'?'

'I'm fine. What do you know?'

'Nuthin',' came Aadje's standard offering to the question regularly asked whenever the friends met up. What it lacked in narrative, was more than compensated for in brevity.

As Aadje and Peter wend their way to school, they are joined by a cascade of youngsters, like sugar ants swarming to the nectar, on their way to the tabernacle of enlightenment, fun, laughter and hard-knocks. Aadje ran his regular gauntlet of sneers and jeers from Blackie and his praetorian guard. With eyes averted and head down, Aadje just quickened his pace and darted to his locker, leaving Peter to wallow in his wake.

'Why do you hang around with that Dutch kid, he's useless? You'd be better off finding some decent friends.' These were the taunts levelled at Peter, as he too, shuffled up the steps to his locker.

'He's alright. Leave him alone,' was Peter's feeble and only response, as he departed their company as quickly as his crutches and callipered legs would allow.

'You wouldn't have anything to do with clogs if you weren't

a cripple. So run away and snivel like he does,' screamed the taunt that hurt Peter most. Unsure whether the emotion he felt was sympathy for Aadje, or a rush of self-pity brought on by the slur that belittled his mobility. Peter, teary and despondent, made his pained way through the milling throng and to the solitude of his locker. Little did Peter know, and therefore could deride no comfort, that Blackie had backhanded his loud mouth acolyte and warned him that calling Devereau a cripple would see him dropped on his arse.

'I'm sorry, Blackie. It just slipped out.' Smidge, quieted by chagrin and embarrassment, promised it would never happen again.

'It had better not. Devereau can't help it if the polio got him. Clogs is different. Devereau can't fight. Kuiper can, but he's just too gutless to take us on.' Blackie's epistle to his mates, in saying it all, brooked no opposition or discussion. Blackie Gavin, a hero to the young locals who gravitated to his sporting prowess, strength, power and protection, had dived off Curlin's Bridge the summer before. His audience of wannabe's and apostles confirmed his daring feat and spread the word to all and sundry as the *gospel* of the righteous and the brave. A feat achieved with the assistance of strategically placed *nit keepers* who kept lookout for the local constabulary and signalled the all clear to dive. Sgt O'Reilly had for many a long time, tried in vain to catch the dare devils flaunting safety and the law by diving from Curlin's Bridge and its lofty perch into the river below. O'Reilly knew, as did the whole of Bowater, that this right-of-passage for the town's young bucks had been a regular summer activity since the bridge was first built ninety odd years ago. Trying to catch the miscreants was the sergeant's preoccupation during the summer hiatus, but he readily grasped the futility of his endeavours and trusted that the signage posted at either end of the bridge warning of the dangers of diving into the river below would, at least, deter some with more sense than bravado. For Blackie Gavin, it was a symbol of manhood with the added bonus of cementing his heroic status among his sycophantic disciples, growing congregation of worshippers and the young ladies of the district.

As Aadje's winter of discontent dragged on, he and Peter entertained themselves with drifting aimlessly around town and explored the iconic river that quarantined Bowater's privileged from the scourge of the troglodytes massing in the east. During these times, Aadje often expressed his despair in carrying a name that honoured his Dutch heritage.

'If I had an English name, maybe Blackie would leave me alone,' was his regular grievance. Their friendship was glued with these meanderings where, left to their own devices, the two discards shunned by the mores of a society lacking empathy and finesse, found soul mates in each other. Aadje cared for Peter, never asking him to hurry up, helping him over obstacles and cajoling him into ever more daring feats of exploration and adventure. Peter both envied and pitied Aadje. He envied Aadje's two good legs, but mourned his lack of friends and family comforts. On their travels, Aadje would often stop in front of Rowley's sports store and, for long periods of time, drool over the Malvern Star bicycle taking up pride of place in the front window. The price tag put it well out of Aadje's reach, who could no more than covetously gape at the apparition of freedom, knowing he could never have the luxury of owning such a classy machine. Down the street, Bowater Motorcycles and Repairs, resplendent with a showroom glistening with new BSA's, Ariels and Triumphs beckoned the adventurous and the thrifty. Aadje regularly stopped and ogled the icons of emancipation, absorbing the array of machinery bathed in chrome and pinstripe.

'One day I'll have me one of them,' he would say to Peter, who recognised the hope in Aadje's voice and the futility of his own longing.

Occasionally, Peter would accompany Aadje and his ferrets while he did a spot of rabbiting. Aadje regularly brought home a rabbit or two for his mum to supplement their sometimes spartan dinner of vegetables from Chen Kwong's market garden. A welcome gift from a redoubtable oriental that, while small in stature, was big in heart, faith, hope and charity. Peter enjoyed rabbiting with Aadje and his ferrets. He grinned in awe as the ferrets drove the unfortunate rabbit into the net and Aadje's deft use of soap to deter the fangs of an excited ferret averse to being collared for its trip home. Rarely did Aadje need to dig out a warren to retrieve a recalcitrant ferret determined to stake its flag in a quarry's former abode. Rabbits came to this part of Victoria in the 1860's and quickly multiplied to plague proportions. Destroying pasture and causing erosion as they, like the early settlers, colonised large tracts of arable land and became a pest to pastoralist and drover alike. The status of the humble rabbit was elevated, albeit temporarily, when in times of economic desperation, they provided food for the working dogs of the district, those on strike, the unemployed, the homeless and the destitute. The depressions of the 1890's and 1930's and the taint of hardship were mitigated somewhat by the rabbit whose sacrifice, supplemented by the odd duffed lamb, opened the door to salvation and gave sustenance to the disadvantaged.

The boys would often come across Chen as he hawked his vegetables door to door throughout the township. Garnering what little money he earned in the process. With a bow and a smile, he would regale them with the gospel according to Confucius and the stricture to be good. He would, then, wave them on their way with a gift from his wares. With carrot in hand, the boys would continue their adventure, leaving Chen Kwong to the uncertainty of his round. And so was the passage of their days. Aadje running washing when needed, the travails of Bowater Higher Elementary, the barrage of barbs from Blackie and his vassals and wandering the entrails of a township racked with division, guilt and charm.

Winter found Devereau weighted by ripples of regret in letting down his Engineer, and his failure to manoeuvre Council into choosing an appropriate site for the new landfill. His fumbling apology to Dawson for his lack of support had not palliated his conscience, nor provided much in the way of comfort for his senior officer unceremoniously rolled by Council. He had been found wanting on a pivotal issue of town planning and was not comfortable in the skin of a chameleon. His days were taken up with administering the operations of his Council, fending off intermittent, often vociferous, objection to the location of the proposed rubbish tip and in preparation for the closing and capping of the old landfill. His Engineer had begun work on excavating the site at the end of Jackson's Road, with the security fencing already installed. A knock at the door saw Dawson glide into his office, hard hat dangling from the end of a sleeveless arm.

'G'day, Andy. How's it going?'

'I'm getting a lot of grief from some of the locals over the new tip and I'll be glad when the bloody thing's operational,' Dawson replied.

'Won't we all,' is all Devereau could get out.

'You know we're gonna have to seal Jackson's Road sooner or later, otherwise the dust will smother everyone living in the street and cover half the town if we don't.'

'Yeah! I agree. But it will have to be referred to estimates and it will be at least eighteen months before we'll have the budget for a seal,' Devereau explained, looking up at the lithe figure of the Shire's Engineer.

'Gravel and water might help in the short term. Can I go ahead and lay some during spring out of contingency funds. During summer I'll use the water trucks to dampen down the dust,' was the best compromise Dawson could offer.

'Alright. Can you give me some costings and I'll shuffle some monies around to cover it?'

'Consider it done Bill. Will you back me on the sealing of Jackson's Road when I raise it at Council?' quizzed his Engineer, in a tone singed with scepticism and suspicion.

'You have my guarantee on that,' came Devereau's firm commitment.

'Okay then. I'll get back to the site and check progress. Barring bad weather, the tip should be ready to go by the first week in December,' were Dawson's last words as he strode from the Shire Secretary's office and into the foyer.

Devereau could hear the clerk in agitated conversation with someone who was clearly a disgruntled ratepayer over the new tip. His Engineer walked straight into Mr Murphy's ambush who, while waving a copy of the *Bowater Bugle*, was regaling all and sundry with shards of venom and vitriol. He was railing against all things Council, the gremlins trolling the corridors of power and the treatment of residents as second-class citizens not worthy of good government.

'You bastards ought to be crucified,' were the last words Devereau heard as he chose to leave his clerk and Engineer to their own devices, and quietly shutting his heavy office door slid silently behind the safety and security of his desk. The last bulwark between him and an unforgiving ratepayer hell bent on making his feelings known. A copy of that day's *Bugle* sat on the corner of his desk.

'I had better have a read,' he thought.

In an unusually hard-hitting news story, rife with satire and under the banner headline, '*Not in My Backyard says Councillors*,' the *Bugle* derided Council's decision to site the new landfill in Jackson's Road, Bowater East, as an inferior site to that of the one on the southern outskirts of town. The editorial questioned the Council's motives and suggested self-interest to be the driving force behind the decision. Not to mention the unseemly haste to cap the old tip and open the new. Perhaps, the paper suggested, the haste was designed to take the heat out of the growing controversy and stall opposition in its dusty tracks. Council, the *Bugle* postulated, wants the landfill issue killed off and forgotten so that the good name of the municipality and the reputation of its councillors will remain untainted by guile and accusations of vested interest.

Winter drifted toward August, which saw Devereau at his desk in a flurry of activity, ignoring as best he could the bubbling cauldron of angst and demands that raged powerlessly in the pubs and echoed up and down the canyons of a town mired deep in cynicism. This, to spite the *Bugle* which, in the week following the original editorial mocking Council's landfill decision, issued a clarification, if not an abject retraction of its story. The lengthy article highlighted the deficiencies of the southern site as a tip and expressing support for Council's reasoning on the selection of Jackson's Road as the better of the two alternatives. The retraction, when it came saw a grin break out on Devereau's visage. For within a day of the original story's publication he had heard on the municipal grapevine that the two councillors who supported the Jackson's Road site, and whose extensive business interests gave them considerable economic clout, had visited the editor and reminded him of how much advertising they threw at the *Bugle*. Their none too subtle hint that a retraction would be in the best financial interest of the paper got his undivided attention and, as they explained, would clear his mind of confusion. Their active involvement and influence in Bowater's Business Association was added incentive for the paper's editor to massage the story and make peace with the disgruntled merchants and their threats of menace. At the time, Devereau shook his head in wonder at democracy in action and grinned in awe with the realisation that the power of the press was no match for the might of a Council scorned.

'Bugger the little people. The sultans of commerce will do over the fourth estate every time. Mustn't let facts get in the way of a good story, or, indeed contradict Council's resolve,' thought Devereau, as he filed the edition away.

With spring in the air, Devereau was active in preparing September's Statutory meeting of Council. Where following a brief meeting, budget estimates would be approved and a new Shire President elected. At this meeting the rates, revenues and expenditure would be set for the next financial year. Including, the development costings for the main street beautification plans, establishing fees for the new tip and the sealing of Jackson's Road, together with a myriad of minor works covering street lighting, signage, footpaths and animal control. The Shire's pound needed expansion and monies set aside for the design work for a new bridge over the Daraleet River. Not to mention the need for new road making plant and equipment. The government was rumbling over the cost of maintaining its railway passenger service from Bowater to Melbourne and was threatening to close the service if patronage did not improve. From Devereau's perspective, all requested reports had been presented to Council at previous meetings and the September meeting should translate as a straight forward affair. It was likely that Cyril Dixon would be re-elected Shire President. Who, after 27 years on Council and 9 as Shire President, was seeking consecutive one year terms in the Presidential robes. Cr Curlin, who felt entitled, was lobbying hard for election as Deputy Shire President. Curlin was in his sixties and carried his age well. Lean and lithe like a cat on the prowl, he, wizened and tanned, was a rustic canvas edged in a gilded frame crafted by toil and entitlement. It showed a man who spent much time tilling the soil and defending his broad dominion from heresy and the barbarians skulking in the shadows of sinister intent. Cr Curlin found threat under every bushel of wheat he harvested and mortared the ramparts of his being with power, privilege and the judicious application of the legal process. Devereau and his officers, while not keen on Dixon's re-election, resigned themselves to the inevitable and went about business as usual. Dixon's rural conservatism, where tight fiscal control is more important than services, manacled the Shire to state and Commonwealth government largesse in the form of grants for the expansion of major infrastructure development. Cr Dixon had long been characterised as a mill stone around the neck of progress by friend and foe alike.

For the Shire President, lean budgets, low rates, good roads and clean streets were the panacea of good governance, with state and federal jurisdictions responsible for everything else. Devereau's proposed budget estimates risked Dixon's ire in the context of projected increased expenditure on capital works and township improvements. Devereau, with a shrug, was about to throw his planning credentials on the table and hoped that enough of the remaining councillors would bite the bullet and grasp the need to drag Bowater, kicking and screaming, out of the 1890's and into the 1950's.

'May the cards fall where they do,' was Devereau's laconic approach to the task at hand. 'Progress comes at a cost,' he reasoned.

For Devereau and his Engineer, the meeting went better than expected. While Cr Dixon was re-elected President, much of Devereau's budget was ratified by Council. With gavel in hand, the Shire President, with barely disguised annoyance and much misgiving, passed each resolution on a show of hands. Attempts by Crs Clark and Keegan to raise the landfill issue were promptly ruled out of order and discussion terminated by the wooden echo of a gavel wielded by an artefact that brooked no opposition. While Dixon, being a patriarch of the old conservative rural school, had reservations over the new budget, his business brethren had no such qualms. Seeing growth and development as synonymous with profit, they were able to cajole enough of their rural colleagues, Curlin included, in support of the new financial regime, roll the numbers and carry the day.

The only surprise, concerning as it was to Devereau, related to a resolution calling on the Engineer to prepare a report on the viability, cost and effectiveness of raising the height of the weir to capture more water for the town. Coming out of left field as it did, Devereau was a little nonplussed as to why the matter hadn't been raised with him and, given the landfill debacle, wondered about the motives behind the request. Still, the meeting ended with Devereau experiencing an elation he had not felt for some time. In response to the government's veiled threat to close the town's passenger service, Council resolved to organise, at its next meeting, a delegation to the Minister for Transport to press the case for retaining the service.

For Aadje and Peter, as for his father, winter had morphed into spring. Their wanderings over the past few months transgressed into September's Bowater Agricultural show. Held on the first Saturday in September, the show first saw light in 1865 with the formation of the Agricultural Society. The show developed over time to become the calendar highlight of the year for the Shire and local community. Arts, crafts, cattle, sheep, horses and Miss Show Girl all vied for popularity with the various sideshows and entertainment. Alby O'Dwyer thrilled the crowds on the main arena with his skill as a horseman and inspirational trick riding. All performed for the throngs of spectators as he galloped at break neck speed around the oval. Rocky Harmer's boxing tent, brightly adorned with murals of pugilists in action, opened for business with the pounding of the bass drum to attract customers to the next bout between his troupe of indigenous boxers and some local hero. At the centre of all this pugnacious attention was Rocky himself, who would, by prearranged decree, provoke a compliant and well-known local into a bout with well-chosen invective belittling his manhood, courage, boxing ability or big mouth. With the drum pounding a sinister and provocative tattoo, paying customers would pour into the tent to watch the local take on one of Harmer's highly credentialed fighters. Little did the crowd realise that the fights, and the result, were choreographed. Gloves were bigger and softer than regulation championship gloves, with their fists balled up inside so that they slapped rather punched each other. Invariably, the local won the first bout, which prompted the challenge of a rematch. And, as preordained, a rematch was duly held while crowds, fired by Harmer's eloquent threats of pugilistic mayhem, flocked to the entertainment and the prospect of a local giving one of Harmer's boys a hiding. Two Bowater lads, Billy and Bluey Aldous, Golden Glove boxers of some ability, were two such locals. Well known to Rocky, they would, as arranged, lurk around the tent until they were publicly challenged to take on one of the troupe's champions. Shamed into accepting the challenge, they would tackle Harmer's best, with both having multiple fights on the day. At show's close, Billy and Bluey would be found enjoying a quiet beer and a laugh in Rocky's tent with his indigenous pugilists for company. Whereupon, a five-pound note would be handed to each with a cheerful, 'good stuff, boys. I'll see you next year then,' from the man himself. The highlight of the show for Aadje was watching the boxing and dreaming of one day being able to fight his way out of poverty and discontent. Aadje would commingle with the crowd forging its way into the tent and, with guile and a confidence camouflaged by the crush of numbers, glide through undetected and without paying. It was only when numbers attracted to the bout were down, that Aadje could not muster the courage to sneak in. Aadje, who used his secret crossing to spirit himself into the showgrounds free of charge, caught up with Peter at the boxing tent, and together took in the sights and sounds of the arena, the animal pavilions and the sideshows. For some reason, unknown to Peter at the time, Aadje was adamant in his refusal to enter the canine pavilion or watch the sheep dog trials. At show's end, the two friends parted. Covered in dust, weary with excitement and hungry they made their way home. Peter, a little slower and wearier than Aadje, lost sight of his mate as the crowds streamed through the double wrought iron gates and into the bowels of Bowater and district.

The show passed and the two friends resumed meandering whenever it fitted in with Aadje's need to run washing around town for his mother. It was one day after school in late September. Aadje was, this fateful day, carrying a full basket of freshly washed and ironed clothes down the main street of Bowater to Mrs Fuller's house when Blackie launched himself from a shop front door way and elbowed Aadje in the ribs as he passed. The momentum of the strike caused Aadje to drop the basket of washing. With clothes scattered all over the footpath, Blackie and his two ruffians proceeded to kick them across the path and into the gutter. Aadje, with a cry of despair, yelled, 'why'd you do that? That's me mum's washing you've ruined. I'll get into big trouble.'

'Serves you right. You weakling. Why don't you go home where you belong?' Blackie sniggered. A snigger interrupted by the bellow of the beast.

'What do you think you're doing, you little animals. Get outta here before I give you a good foot in the behind,' an angry Bill Devereau ranted. His face reddened with rage, provided all the incentive Blackie and his accomplices needed to bolt for their lives.

'Aadje, isn't it? Are you alright?' asked Devereau, still shaking with anger and with gritted teeth he picked up the washing from the footpath and gutter. Aadje, with tears streaming down his cheeks, was frozen to the spot.

'It's okay, Aadje. I'll drive you home and explain everything to your mum. I'm sure she'll understand.' With washing basket under one arm, Devereau gently led a sobbing Aadje to his car. Through tears of hurt and frustration, Aadje kept reciting, 'why do they do this to me? Why can't they leave me alone? I don't do anything to them.' Stopping in front of Anki's house, Devereau, washing in hand, explained what had happened and that it wasn't Aadje's fault.

'Why do they do this to my boy?' A woeful Anki cried, wringing her hands in frustration and distress.

'Unfortunately, Mrs Kuiper, some wear the bridle of

superiority as a god given right to bully,' replied Devereau, still angry and determined to set matters right.

'Look. If you give me the address, I'll go and explain to the lady what had happened and let her know you'll have her clothes to her in the next day or so.'

'You're a good man, Mr Devereau. Mrs Fuller is at 23 Highgrove Street. It would help a lot if you could do that for me. I'd have to walk it and as you can see Aadje needs me right now.'

'I'm happy to help Mrs Kuiper,' Devereau replied. With a hand gently placed on Aadje's shoulder, Devereau growled, 'don't worry son. They'll get theirs one day. I'll see to that.'

'Thankyou Mr Devereau. You're too kind,' was all Anki could utter.

'No problem. I'm happy to help,' Devereau proffered as he got behind the wheel of his Ford Prefect and made his way to Mrs Fuller's house.

'They'll get theirs, I promise you young fella,' he thought, as his mind turned inexplicably to October's Council meeting and an issue or two of concern to him, the community and to decency.

Mrs Fuller, while a little put out, understood the situation after Devereau had outlined what had happened in the street.

'The poor kid. That'll be okay, it'll get here sooner or later. Tell Anki not to worry,' voiced Mrs Fuller, her words of sympathy and understanding calming, just a little, Devereau's thinly veiled anger.

On the way home, he paid a visit to Sgt O'Reilly to report Blackie and his fellow transgressors as being menaces that need a good talking to. Sgt O'Reilly, already aware of the matter, indicated to Devereau that Mrs Rowley had witnessed the whole scenario from her sports shop and had reported it to the local police.

'I'll go around and visit the young lad and his dad tonight. He's become too big for his boots since he dived off the bridge. He was bad news before, but the little show off has got worse. I'll have a word with his father. I expect that as the manager of the milk factory he doesn't want his smart aleck son giving him a bad name around town,' the sergeant intoned.

'That's great,' Devereau chuckled, relishing the thought that Blackie would, at long last, get his just deserts. 'In that case, I'll leave the matter in your capable hands to deal with.'

'Don't worry Bill. I'll fix it,' finished O'Reilly as Devereau slid into his car for the short drive home.

Sinister Intent

As ordained, Aadje and Peter met up at Curlin's Bridge and straggled their way to the front gates that welcomed them to the school of their perfidy. By planned coincidence, their entry was trumpeted by the clang of the school bell that reverberated through the still morning air. Like all the days that had gone before, Blackie, Curly, Ginger and Smidge formed a welcoming committee gifted with malice and, through belief in a myth of their own making, righteousness. As Aadje passed through the gates of his discontent, Blackie in anger and mock justice, shouldered Aadje from the path and, with a finger stabbing barbs of venom, declared. 'You got us into trouble. O'Reilly talked to me dad. You're a stinkin' no good dobber and we're gonna get you.'

'Yeah! You betta watch out from now on you Dutch rat,' chorused Blackie's cohorts in tyranny.

'He didn't dob. Me dad did so you'd better leave him alone. He's done nothin' to you,' Peter re-joined in genuine sympathy for his friend. Somewhat taken aback by Peter's spirited defence of his friend, Blackie and his apostles, silent with clenched fists balled in odium, glared at Aadje and, with a sideways glance at Peter, melted away to the accolades of their collective delusions awash with moral outrage and basking in the glory of natural superiority. Aadje, teary, thanked his friend for standing up for him and, with a face that bespoke of defiant determination, promised that he would show them. 'One day they'll be sorry. One day…,' his voice trailed off and was lost in the clatter and clutter of a corridor disgorging its contents to the classroom.

Since the September meeting, Devereau had been wracked with disquiet and a sense of foreboding. His budget proposals and strategic plans had been largely accepted and he had the authority to implement a design brief for a new streetscape for the beautification of the town's main thoroughfare. Bowater's gateway to a rural idyll would be paved with opportunity, mortared in progress and cemented with Christian values. Fossicker Street, lined with date palms and hitching posts, with its deep gutters, narrow and broken footpaths, potted asphalt and haphazard parking cried out for a makeover to create a vista worthy of the Shire's motto: *'Prosperity through Toil.'* Fossicker Street was named for the gold prospectors as they wended their way, via the path of least resistance, to and from the gold fields. Originally dubbed Fossicker's Track, the trail embraced progress with gusto as artisans, merchants and charlatans of all stripes set up business to fleece the transients on their way to the diggings. Progress that not only brought wealth, but coaxed the nascent titans of trade to stroke their blossoming narcissistic self-importance and expunge '*Track*' from Bowater's lexicon and history's grand opus. It evoked the primitive, the lowly and the uncivilised and the name was duly consigned to antiquity. Henceforth, Fossicker Street, in its new livery, would, in name and deed, became the town's high-water mark on its trek to the promised land. Its majesty sealed for ever when the *Bowater Roads' District* installed a sign post anointing Fossicker Street with new found status. Its verandah'd vista had faded over time. A once richly coloured and vibrant canvas, enamelled in prosperity, hope and entitlement, had rusted, stagnant, in the cycle of economic boom and bust. A two-act operetta that dampened confidence, softened enthusiasm and tempered caution. Now all it needed was some tender massaging to establish a streetscape so alluring that patrons would arrive in droves and the web of commerce could then, with cunning aforethought, ensnare all who dared enter its beatified precincts. Devereau smiled at the thought of introducing parking bays into the main street and ruminated on how the locals would adapt to an innovation foreign to their way of being. For Devereau understood that the only lines this community accepted was the one in the sand that dared any one to cross. The habit of parking their cars and trucks at any angle that suited, created a street scene chaotic in appearance and risky in manoeuvre. 'It will be interesting,' was all Devereau could voice when questioned on how his proposed new regime would work. Of greater concern to Devereau was the request for a report on raising the weir on the Daraleet. He harboured grave reservations over the proposal. Not only was he suspicious of the motives driving the resolution, but the impact it would have on those occupying the banks of the river upstream from the weir. An anxiety brokered in the realisation that he, as Shire Secretary, had been quarantined from the request and his counsel not sought.

'I'll have a yarn to Andy about this,' Devereau noted and returned to the mundane occupying his municipal desk. A few days earlier he had met the local RSL branch to plan for November 11 and Remembrance Day at the town's War Memorial. With the day still three weeks away, he could report that all was in readiness for the 11:00 am service, including seating and refreshments for the attending dignitaries, including the local Member of Parliament, the keynote speaker, Major General Holgate (Ret.) and the officiating clergy. A number of Council staffers, returned servicemen all, would be involved, including Andy Dawson, who, following his graduation from Melbourne University, enlisted in 1943 as a twenty-three-year-old and saw active service in the Middle East and New Guinea.

His reflective melancholia was disturbed by a sharp knock at his door which, upon swinging open, presented him with the spectre of his Engineer striding towards his desk. Barely containing his glee, Andy swanned into the vacant chair in front of Devereau and blurted out the reason for his visit.

'You might not have heard yet, but last night someone dumped rubbish all over Cr Ferguson's front yard. He's as mad as a cut snake and wants the town scoured for the criminal element who would dare treat a man of his standing with so much disrespect,' gossiped the nearly breathless Shire Engineer.

'It'd be over the landfill site and someone's decided they wouldn't get mad, they'd get even. Poetic justice of sorts I'd say. What's been done about it?' Devereau questioned.

'Ferguson called Sgt O'Reilly who, with a flourish of self-importance, promptly declared his front yard a crime scene to keep the councillor and his family away from his evidence while he played detective. O'Reilly called me over this morning to witness the mess and indicated that he and his constable had searched the garbage and asked Council to remove it as quickly as possible. He's a cunning fox that one. I noted a crumpled envelope fell out of his pocket while we talked. He, with his foot, drew the envelope to him and stood on it while he encouraged me to take my leave. The envelope had a name and address on it, so I s'pose he will follow that where ever it takes him,' narrated Dawson, consumed with mirth.

'Well, we knew there'd be trouble over this. I just hope this is the last of it. So, the rubbish is gone and Ferguson's madder than hell and the good sergeant is on the case,' noted Devereau, barely camouflaging the triumph in his voice.

'Yep. That's right,' said his Engineer. 'Cr Ferguson and the Council have galvanised some serious hostility and we're now the focus of a fair whack of disaffection and, while I shouldn't be saying it, some of them rightfully deserve all that comes their way,' chortled Dawson.

'Let's hope O'Reilly's mind is closed for repairs during his quest for the culprit,' shot back a grinning Devereau. 'But, tell me Andy, what's with this proposition to raise the level of the weir and the report Council asked you to prepare for next week's Council meeting?'

'Look Bill, I haven't finished the report and before I did, I wanted to catch up with you to fill you in on what's going on. So now's as good a time as any,' Andy stressed, all mirth now gone.

The Engineer walked his Shire Secretary through the maze of shabby motives and political intrigue attached to the call to lift the height of the town's weir. It appears that Steve Adair, during summer, makes a nice little sandy beach at the bottom of his yard so his kids can swim in the river away from Bowater's lesser lights using the town's swimming hole near the bridge. Adair, who owns the local hardware, wants to have the height raised because each winter the river level rises from rain in the catchment and overflows the weir. As his property is downstream, the winter overflow washes his beach away and every summer, so it is claimed, he needs to replace the sand at considerable cost in time and money.

'The problem we have is that he got in the ear of his close mates Crs Curlin and McNichol, who are now pushing for a lift in the weir's height. At the mention of McNichol's name, Devereau, raising his eyebrows and hackles at the same time, and through lips taut with anger, let out an incredulous, 'What? Besides the fact that Adair's got no right building a private beach on a river that doesn't belong to him, what impact will it have?' questioned an exasperated Shire Secretary. With nary a pause, his Engineer continued to explain that any rise in weir height will bank the river back further upstream and flood some of Kwong's market garden.

'You're kiddin' me, aren't you? Have these people no shred of decency or honour?' was all that Devereau, shaking his head, could muster as cold, grey fury consumed him.

'Bill, Curlin and McNichol are looking after their mate. For them morals and decency take a back seat when it comes to helping out a friend. We don't run this place you know. The gang of six own this town and they're in the pockets of each other. My report will recommend referring it to committee with the view to burying it. It's my only gambit. But I know that my recommendation will get voted down at Council,' declared the Engineer, with an air of resignation.

'Do they have support?' questioned Devereau.

'Like I said, they are part of the Council clique who run this town.'

'What about Freeman?'

'I dunno Bill. But after he opposed their landfill motion, he owes them a favour and because it doesn't affect his Riding, he's likely to fall into line,' was all Andy could add.

'Ah! It's a pity Mr Kwong isn't a Protestant. What's their justification? I expect it will be riddled with mischief, while pandering to common sense and local sensitivities,' groaned an increasingly despondent Devereau.

'They want a bigger pondage to guard against the ravages

of drought. They didn't make any mention of a private beach,' Andy declared.

'We can't even accuse them of deceit, the fraudulent bastards. Their resolution will relate to the weir and not their mate. Where's the *State Rivers and Water Supply Commission* stand on this Andy?'

Dawson reported that his initial inquiry to the SRWSC indicated that, while they have yet to conduct a thorough evaluation of the proposition, they don't see, on the surface, any problems so long as the weir is only lifted by eighteen inches at most. 'That would back the water up around three hundred yards and cover up part of Kwong's garden, making it unviable and cutting off his current access. Cr Curlin wants the resolution to go through Council at its October meeting so work can begin, and be complete, before the onset of winter rains,' asserted Dawson.

'Did you know about the beach Andy?' queried Devereau.

'Yeah! I did. But I chose to turn a blind eye knowing that every winter, poetic justice visited the Adair's and washed away their beach. To tackle them on it would only have caused problems that weren't worth the fight.'

'I understand, Andy. I know where you're coming from and, given their clout, I would probably have done the same thing. Well, I suppose at least Keegan and Clark won't support them out of principle and an unbridled distrust of the gentry running this municipality. How Freeman votes is irrelevant given the healthy majority the others have. Are these people for real? Don't they care who they hurt?' growled

Devereau, agitation etching deep into his scowling forehead. Andy, dispirited and looking his boss squarely in the eye, said, 'you know Bill, vested interest has no boundaries and no morals. The town is littered with the bones of its victims.'

'Oh, well Andy. The index of discord is about to rise. We got the landfill, now the weir. We're in for a fun ride. Take care, I'll catch you later,' were Devereau's parting words to his Engineer as Dawson left his office.

Sergeant O'Reilly's ample girth stood leaning on the front gate of Tom Murphy's Jackson's Road cottage. With effort he opened the gate and shambled up the narrow footpath to the front door. Standing, wedged, between the pot plants guarding Mr Murphy's battered cottage portal, O'Reilly knocked with all the authority his senior sergeant stripes could muster.

'G'day Sergeant,' came a voice from somewhere within the darkened bowels of the corridor. 'What do I owe the pleasure of this visit?'

'I think you know Tom. There's this little problem of rubbish chucked all over Cr Ferguson's front yard,' claimed the sergeant through laboured breath.

'Know nuthin' about it sarge. That's not my style and, besides, he's not worth the effort,' was Murphy's less than offended defence. Sgt O'Reilly, with a sigh, reached into his pocket and withdrew a crumpled envelope. In a motion slowed by his love of melodrama, O'Reilly smoothed the envelope of guilt and read to Mr Murphy the address, stained but legible, with an air of smug satisfaction.

'Mr T. Murphy, 23 Jackson's Road, Bowater East.' O'Reilly, holding up the evidence for Tom Murphy to read, said in an accusatory voice, 'this is one of your letters and it was among the rubbish in the councillor's front yard. Tom, you need to be more careful.'

'Oh, that. I must have dropped it in the street and it's blown into Ferguson's front yard by accident Bill,' rambled Murphy, whose lame explanation for his errant envelope was lost on O'Reilly.

'Tom. Don't piss on me leg and tell me it's raining. I know you did the deed and it's because I sympathise with you poor buggers in this street that I want to bury the matter.' O'Reilly, holding his Sword of Damocles aloft, uttered, 'this is the only piece of evidence anyone's got and I'll give it over if you give me your word you won't try any more of these silly stunts. It'll land you in big trouble if you do,' snapped the senior sergeant, basking in the aura of the sage.

'Alright Bill. I'm not saying I did it mind you, but if it makes you happy, you have my word. Somebody's gotta stand up to them councillors who think they own the town and can treat us like dirt,' gritted Murphy, surrendering to the power and majesty of a senior sergeant who, this day, was taking no prisoners.

'I know what you're saying Tom, but I can't have you taking the law into your own hands. And, it doesn't look good if I can't solve the case. Here's your envelope. Burn the bloody thing,' uttered a breathless Sgt O'Reilly, wearing an acre of smile.

'Thanks Bill. You won't have to worry. There is more than one way to skin a cat.'

'Just make sure it's legal. You pull this stunt again and I'll do you for something more serious,' was O'Reilly's parting threat as he nodded towards Mr Murphy's back shed. Watching the rotund figure of the sergeant squeeze through the open front gate, a mischievous smile crossed Murphy's lips as he gazed at his envelope of perdition and tore it into little pieces. 'Silly me,' he thought, as he pocketed the shards of his undoing. 'That could have been someone else's envelope.'

Devereau sat at his desk, the *Bowater Bugle* laid out before him. He read with a degree of satisfaction the banner headline, '*Councillor Target of Rubbish Attack*'. The story, together with a grainy photograph of the crime scene, described the wilful dumping of rubbish in Cr Ferguson's front yard in the early hours of Tuesday morning. 'The cowardly perpetrators, under cover of darkness, destroyed the peace and good order of Bowater with their dastardly crime,' screamed the *Bugle*. 'Cr Ferguson claims his support for the new landfill in Bowater East was the motive behind the attack. But that he wouldn't be intimidated by any person with evil on their mind, trumpeted the *Bugle*. The report went on to say that Ferguson had expressed concern for his family, but was confident police would crack the case and bring the miscreants to justice. According to the *Bugle,* Sgt O'Reilly is investigating the matter and is following a number of promising leads. While no arrests have been made as yet, Sgt O'Reilly told the *Bugle* that his inquiries were continuing and was hopeful of solving the case in the not too distant future. 'My how the worm turns,' reflected Devereau as his mind cast back to the *Bugle's* very first public tirade over the landfill issue. Only to be pulled back into line by the threats of councillors scorned. Devereau smiled as he pondered the article and wondered how much O'Reilly was really committed to finding the phantom of the night who embraced civil disobedience as the weapon of choice against the injustices of the world. After carefully folding the *Bugle* and dispatching it to a vacant corner of his desk, Devereau called Millie and asked her to arrange a meeting with Crs Owen and McNichol for some time next week. 'Before October's Council meeting on the twenty third,' he instructed. 'Will do,' noted Millie, cheerful as always.

It was a Saturday morning when Aadje and Peter met up for their regular exploration of the river bank. There they could enjoy the company of each other and far from the trials and tribulations of a world massed against them. When they were together Peter felt whole. His callipered legs and crutches faded to a challenge, rather than an anchor of hindrance and where, in the solitude of the Daraleet's meander, they could bathe in the freedom only true friendship bequeaths. The river gums, willows and peppercorns guarded the turbid waters that carried the hopes and dreams of a community in conflict with itself. Harmony was the surface, contradiction the psychosis. The river, tranquil in its flight through the hinterland, was, for the two friends, a ribbon of comfort that shielded them from the caprice that is life's discord. In the distance, a lonely figure was massaging the cricket club's turf wicket with a mechanical roller that was pummelling the Merri Creek clay into submission.

'Hey, Peter. Look there's a swaggie asleep under that willow. His dog's with him,'

Yeah! He must be tired,' Peter added, without any real excitement.

Moving closer, the two boys could see an old man slumped against the tree and close to the river's run. Grey beard, torn jacket, dirty dungarees and boots without laces defined his repose. His swag was laid out beside him, while his dog, whimpering, lay across his outstretched legs. As they drew ever nearer, the swaggie's kelpie lifted its head and let out a short-muffled growl. Stopping dead in their tracks, Aadje called out, 'hey, mister. You awake?' With no answer, Aadje repeated the effort. 'Hey, mister! Are you alright?' The Kelpie, animated by the boys' efforts to waken the old man, snarled deeper in response to the renewed threat to its master. The swaggie's eyes were half closed, mouth ajar with saliva matting his nicotine flecked beard. Aadje looked at Peter and in a voice laden with realisation murmured, 'hey Peter. I think the old fella's dead.'

'Do you reckon?' gasped Peter, now quivering with the excitement of the unknown. Aadje, picking up a stick, underarmed it in the direction of the old fellow to test the accuracy of his assessment, if not his arm. The Kelpie, taking umbrage at the assault on its master, got to its feet and, with hackles up, barked a warning to back off. The boys, frozen to the spot, stared at the lifeless form of society's forgotten one until the kelpie's guttural snarl brought them back to stark reality.

'What'll we do now?' questioned Peter, in a voice shrilling with unease. 'I dunno,' was Aadje's first response. 'You stay here and I'll run over and get that bloke rolling the pitch to come see.'

'I'm not stayin' here on my own,' stated Peter, in a tone laden with concern and alarm.

'Alright. You come with me, but I'll run ahead and meet you on the way back.'

Peter struggled as best he could to keep up with Aadje, who got to the oval well ahead of his battling, trembling cobber. Aadje, still some distance from the bloke and his mechanical beast working over the wicket, yelled over the rumble of the roller, 'hey mister. We need your help. We need to show you something. I think it's bad.'

Somewhat surprised, the young man, his cricket cap propped jauntily on his head, shut down his roller and asked, 'what's up kid?'

'There's a swaggie down by the river and I think he's dead,' was all Aadje could blurt out. The young man jumped the cyclone wire fence that sundered the cricket ground from the outside world and, in a brisk trot, headed in the direction of Aadje's extended arm. Collecting a struggling Peter on the way, they approached the site of the old man's apparent demise. The young man, stick in hand, swung it at the head of the snarling kelpie and poking the old man in the side, said, without emotion, 'yep. He's dead alright. You kids wait here while I go get Sgt O'Reilly. If you step away a bit, you'll be okay until I get back.' The boys waited in silence, unable to avert their gaze from the poor fellow propped up some twenty yards in front of them. The faithful kelpie had resumed its pride of place with its head once more resting on its master's legs. A scene haloed by the dappled shade of the willow that filtered strobes of golden light over the swaggie's pale and matted beard. His battered and sweat stained hat, featuring the suspended corks that defined the genus, lay beside his outstretched arm. In what seemed an aeon, Sgt O'Reilly and the young man finally returned. Followed shortly thereafter by a hearse from A.K. Bromwich's funeral parlour.

'Step back, boys. It might be best if you went home now fellas. You've done all you can do. We'll take care of it from here,' instructed the sergeant. While stepping back, they were reluctant to leave, glued to the second act of a play scripted in tragedy and staged in the theatre of the wretched. From a distance, they could see O'Reilly remove a rifle from his car and, with callous aforethought, put the unfortunate kelpie out of its misery. The swaggie's body, together with his dog, was unceremoniously bundled into the back of the hearse which drew away at, what was to the boys, an unseemly clip. In what was a tribute to efficiency, the river, in a matter of minutes, once more returned to its former serenity. The willow, once again, cast its shadowed fingers across the old man's last resting place. The only remaining monument to his being was the outline of his legs etched in the grass where they had laid. A cairn destined to evaporate in the mists of time and the first hint of wind or rain. Aadje spoke first.

'I wish he hadn't done the dog. I could've had him. It wasn't right.'

'Gee, Aadje. Don't be too upset. Me dad says some dogs are one-man dogs. I don't think that one would take to anyone else. I wish they hadn't shot him though. It's sad. I wanna get out of here now,' Peter finished. The two boys, deep in their own thoughts, made their slow and, now, pained way home to the comfort of mothers who understood love and death.

Peter, with Aadje in tow, arrived home at his place in a state of agitated excitement. Mrs Devereau, on hearing the details of their morning together comforted, as best she could, with milk, biscuits and some kind words. After which Aadje followed Peter to his room where both sat in silence. Aadje thought of his little sister resting peacefully in a white casket, flowers all around, of a mother sobbing and of a father wringing his hands in grief. Up until Jericho Jack, it was the only time he had seen the body of the departed. His sister, her pretty face framed in locks of brown. With her eyes closed, waxen cheeks and pale lips she spoke of the embalmer's art. She was clothed in her favourite dress and a bracelet given to her by a doting family on the eve of her last birthday on earth. With memories flooding back, Aadje closed his eyes against the tears beginning to form and as a shield against the wave of grief descending upon him.

'What's wrong Aadje? Why so quiet?'

'Nuthin'. I gotta go soon. I have to take washing to Mrs Junor for mum and she'll be wondering where I am,' replied Aadje, bathed in a melancholia of bad dreams and lives lost. On his way out Aadje thanked Mrs Devereau for the milk.

'We don't have much milk at home. So thanks Mrs Devereau.' Alice Devereau, consumed by a wave of sympathy, insisted Aadje drink another glass before making his way home. 'Now you make sure you talk to your mum when you get home. She needs to know about your day so she can help if you need some comfort,' cajoled Mrs Devereau, with sympathy welling in her breast.

'Thanks Mrs Devereau. See ya Pete,' were the last words Aadje uttered as he made his way out of the house and into the street. The smell of jacaranda and bottle brush wafted him over Curlin's Bridge and onto the dusty track to his home in Jackson's Road. Peter, who had followed Aadje into the kitchen, stood silent watching his mother rinsing the glasses. Wiping her hands on her apron, she looked up at Peter and in a voice laced with tenderness asked, 'are you alright son? You're very quiet.'

'I'm okay mum. I've never been that close to a dead person before. He looked so peaceful, like he's asleep,' responded Peter.

'If you need to talk son, I'm here and I'm a good listener,' said his mum, full of reassurance. Peter, thinking of the bodies he had spied through the cracked and murky windows of Bromwich's ramshackle mortuary said, 'yeah! I know mum. I think I'll go outside and sit for a while. I hope Aadje's alright.' His words trailed off as he shuffled his way onto the front verandah.

'He'll be alright. He has his mum and anyway your dad will be home soon and you can have a talk with him,' returned Mrs Devereau, as she began preparing lunch for her family.

Bill Devereau had been down at Pringle's garage having the alternator replaced on the Ford. He knew it was on the way out, but, like all things personal, he had put off getting it fixed. It was only when the fear of his family being stranded overwhelmed his laxity, did he book the car in for its internal surgery. Saturday morning suited him best, for it meant not taking time off work to run the car to the garage and then find the time to pick it up. Besides, Devereau enjoyed his stroll to and from his office and gave him the opportunity to, on occasion, drop in for a quick beer before the pubs closed at six o'clock. A decree that Devereau found to be most civilised. It was, however, a custom more in the flaunting than in the honouring. The CRB workers, when they hit town, are billeted at the only two pubs with accommodation. When the bars shut at six sharp, they would, behind the sanctity of firmly closed doors, continue the amber merriment until they got into mischief and fell upon their beds in an alcohol induced stupor. Word has it that one young buck, well-built, ruggedly handsome and under the influence would, on film nights, ride his 1936 Indian Scout into the foyer of the Strand Theatre and, above the staccato of a growling v-twin, woo the pretty little thing behind the kiosk.

Rumour has it, that the only way this belle could put an end to his two wheeled gallantry was by agreeing to marry him.

Having parked the Ford in the garage, Devereau said, 'g'day,' to Peter on his way past and made his way inside for lunch. 'I'm starving,' was his call to arms. 'Peter seems a bit quiet and reserved,' Devereau noted as he kissed his wife on the forehead. Alice Devereau duly outlined the morning's events and Peter's involvement in the discovery of the dead sundowner.

'Ah! Poor kid. Do you think he'll be okay?' asked Devereau, a ripple of concern trilling his voice.

'He will if he talks about it,' Alice answered.

'I'll spend the afternoon with him and keep his mind off it,' stressed his father.

'No. No. He needs to talk openly about it and how he feels. He can't bottle it up or run away from it if he is to get over the old swaggie's death and accept what's happened,' Mrs Devereau declared.

'Aren't you the shrewd one? I understand. I'll call him in for lunch and we'll talk.' Devereau's words echoed down the passage as he headed for Peter's roost on the front verandah.

Monday for Devereau had started like any other. Council matters were occupying his morning when a knock at his door alerted Devereau to the fact that Millie, true to form, had arranged for him to meet Crs Owen and McNichol. The knock signalled the arrival of the two councillors.

'Come in gentlemen. Take a seat, won't you? Thanks for coming, I know you are both very busy but this shouldn't take too long,' entreated Devereau, as he effusively welcomed the two councillors.

'What's this about?' questioned a terse McNichol. 'I need to be back at the shop.'

'It's about the drive to raise the height of the weir. As you know, it's been agenda'd for next week's Council meeting and I want to gauge the level of Council support for lifting its height prior to the meeting. You know me. I'm not keen on surprises,' humoured Devereau, in a voice laden with determination.

'Sorry Bill, but I don't see the need,' retorted Cr Owen, with just a hint of frustration.

'Oh! I beg to differ. The Engineer tells me that lifting the height of the weir, even by just eighteen inches, will back the water up three hundred yards and flood the Chinaman's market garden. Now gentleman, I don't think that's right or fair,' trolled Devereau, leaning back in his chair.

'We can compensate the Chinaman if need be. We can give him some land somewhere else or pay for the land he's lost,' chorused the two councillors.

'That won't work. He'll lose half his acreage and access to his garden. Besides, there is no council land either available or suitable for him. The only site that might have worked for the Chinaman was the one near the river in Jackson's Road. But, if you remember gentlemen, you turned that into a landfill,' stressed, a now bemused, Devereau.

'The additional pondage is vital for the town's water supply in the long term, and if there is some peripheral damage on the way, so be it,' justified Cr McNichol.

'You realise that the push to raise the weir is my private little beach head,' rasped Devereau, grinning at his subtlety. 'I put it to you councillor, this has little to do with water supply and more to do with Steve Adair's private beach that gets washed away when the winter rains cause the weir to overflow. You are prepared to inflict an injustice on Chen Kwong just so the Adair family can enjoy their very own river front private beach,' scowled Devereau, his pitch brusque with impertinence.

'I find your aspersions on Steve Adair, who has done much for his community, to be offensive and disparaging in the extreme,' moaned Cr Owen, in spirited defence of his mate.

'You've seen nothing yet councillor and that is just my point. It is Steve Adair's community that he benefits, no-one else's. I find your collusion in this tardy affair to be, as you put it councillor, offensive. It is not right, I want the issue to die in committee and I need you to make sure that's exactly what happens,' pronounced Devereau, in a voice that carried as much threat as he could muster.

'Well Bill, we support the raising of the weir and that's the way we'll vote on the night. End of story,' declared Cr McNichol. In a tone sharpened with determination and suppressed anger, Devereau went on to say, 'look I have a proposition that might help you make a more informed decision, one, which would not only be a credit to the community, but of immense personal benefit to you.' The two councillors, leaning forward in expectation, were all ears.

'Go on,' they chirped, like crows coveting a carcass.

'I'm aware of your little picadillo with those two young teachers a little while ago. Half the town is aware of course, but because we closed ranks to protect your precious reputations the rumour mill has gone dead. The dearth of substance and the spreading of false rumours have left the town not knowing what to believe. Now fellas, it's like this. Make sure the weir proposal gets buried and goes way or I'm going to ensure your little late-night trysts are filtered back into the public domain in all their sordid glory. This time, though, the town will be left with no doubt as to who was involved. You see councillors, as Shire Secretary I am duty bound to uphold the integrity of the Shire and the probity of its elected officials. Frequenting a house of ill-repute, gentlemen, is a criminal offence and I would hate to be forced to report my concerns to the relevant state authorities. It is a scandal that, like Lazarus, would rise once more from the dead and pollinate gossip already fertile with mirth and mocking disdain. You'll be, deservedly, the talk in every bar, crevice and cranny throughout the Shire. The whole town will embrace, in all their sordid detail, your little trysts and turns. Your iron shield of silence and denial will turn squalid and rust before your very eyes. Do you read me gentlemen?'

The two councillors, red with silent rage, glared at Devereau and spluttered, 'this is plain blackmail. You can't do this to us and you'll be sorry if you push us too far. We have friends on Council and we'll make sure you are done for if you so much as breathe a word.'

'Come on Councillors. Hardly blackmail. I prefer to describe it as leveraging the best interests of the community. Besides, I might lose my job, but you'll lose a family and a healthy dose of respect. Your reputation will be dirtied by a wave of innuendo and mockery peddled by those in the know. Not to mention what might happen when the matter reaches the big smoke. The cloak of secrecy and obfuscation will be dragged kicking and screaming through the mire of your own making. I don't care how you swing the vote with your friends on Council, that choice is yours gentlemen. But, be aware that if I'm to be removed from this chair, I'll take your precious reputations down with me. The ball's in your court gentlemen. Think carefully on it.' Devereau's, 'good day, councillors,' terminated what was a considerably tension addled, if short, meeting. A parting Cr Owen, rabid with rage, turned and, in a voice basted in venom, reminded Devereau of his station in municipal affairs. 'I'm the past Deputy Shire President and no-one treats me like this. You'll be sorry you ever tried this on. You'll live to regret this,' volleyed a fuming Cr Owen, as he and McNichol stormed from his office.

Shaking with adrenalin fuelled excitement and unable to concentrate, Devereau sat absorbed with a smug satisfaction that comes from a strategic ambush and the exercise of raw power. Not to mention the very real prospect of destroying any vestige of support and the risk of losing his job as Shire Secretary. He was acutely aware of Shakespeare's axiom, *'tempt not a desperate man.'* Since selling out his Engineer and community for job security over the landfill issue, Devereau, through bouts of remorse, had determined that never again would he put self-preservation above what was right. In the silence of his office, overcome with dread and the burden of adversity, Devereau took some cheer from the words of Henry V, '*He that hath no stomach to the fight. Let him depart.*' Devereau, in paying silent homage to the bard and his own leverage file, recognised that he now had two implacable enemies. A number likely to grow as Crs Owen and McNichol set about besmirching his character, faculties and loyalty to their fellow councillors. He for one hadn't worked out his tactics should Owen and McNichol call his bluff. Whatever the outcome, Devereau concluded his career could be spiralling into an abyss of his own creation. A chasm, cleft in piety and gouged with misgiving. A hard-edged reality enveloped him and dampened the euphoria that came with playing councillors at their own game. 'What will be, will be,' he exclaimed to the empty room that was a passive participant in his conspiracy to bring the dogs of injustice to heel. A knock on his door cleared his mind and jolted him back to the present. Millie's dulcet tones had just finished announcing that Cr Freeman wished to see him.

'This can't be good,' the Shire Secretary sighed, as Freeman waltzed into his office. Cr Freeman, on entering Devereau's office, propped himself on a chair opposite and asked how he was going.

'I'm fine, councillor. What can I do for you?'

'You heard, I suppose, about the swaggie they found dead

by the river at the weekend. I understand your young bloke and another kid found the body,' reported Freeman.

'Yeah, that's right. Not very pleasant for anyone. But, Peter's travelling alright. We've talked.'

'That's good. It's sad really. But God works in mysterious ways and the Kingdom of Heaven always awaits the true believers.'

'There's not much mystery about dying councillor,' said Devereau, eyeing the man christened the Crazy Cardinal by the bar flies that regularly downed a few in Bowater's finest. 'How can I help you?' asked Devereau, changing the subject.

'You heard the rumours that the government is giving serious consideration to closing the VR passenger service from here to Melbourne as a cost cutting exercise,' Freeman related.

'It is more than just a rumour councillor. The local government scuttlebutt tells me that Spring Street is poised to act. You know what new governments are like. First, they accuse the old regime of pillaging the state of its wealth, morals and decency, then they slash and burn. Derailing a passenger service in a safe seat like Willaroo is not likely to give the government any heartburn. Cynically, they'll run on the maxim that they are solid money managers who, alone, can get Victoria back on track. While it may come as a surprise and contrary to popular belief, Bowater isn't the centre of the universe and all governments spread their largesse, like manure, where it will do them the most good.'

'That might be so, but Bolte's just fixing the problems caused by Cain and his cronies. We'll save the train, I'm sure.'

'Blaming the last government for the train's poor patronage is a bit over the top Adrian. Passenger numbers have been slowly dropping on the Bowater line for years. As more and more people take to cars, the less they need the train. That's hardly Cain's doing, councillor. What we really need is for the trains to run more often, instead of just the one daily service to the city,' Devereau pontificated, barely managing to suppress the swagger in his voice.

Freeman, ignoring the barbs, explained that he had already spoken to the local member. 'He is concerned as well. This puts him right in the firing line if his government axes the service. He's willing to arrange a Council delegation to meet with the Minister to put our case,' Freeman articulated. 'We would need you to prepare a detailed justification for keeping the passenger service and arrange the meeting.'

'That wouldn't be a problem,' declared Devereau. 'I can fashion a good defence for keeping the passenger train and go with the delegation to argue Council's opposition to closing the service.'

'That's good Bill. I intend to move, at next week's meeting, a resolution for a delegation to meet with the Minister at the earliest opportunity. The motion will ask you to develop a spirited defence of the service. But, Bill, I think it best if only elected councillors met the Minister. The local member agrees that the Minister will be more relaxed, sympathetic and open with the delegation if he isn't confronted by council officers.'

'You know the Minister will have his bureaucrats and

Department Head with him. Priming him, covering his butt and deflecting him from committing to something they don't want him to deliver.'

'I know what you're saying Bill. The local member knows the Minister socially and is adamant that we stand a better chance without any council officers getting in the way. He reckons, based on friendship, he can sway the Minister to review the threatened closure.' 'Okay. It's your Council. As its servant, I'll do what Council directs. Though, I think it would be a mistake to form a delegation without me and the Engineer,' pronounced Deverau, already resigned to the will of Council.

'Alright then. Thanks for your time. We'll see you on the twenty third,' finished Freeman.

'Sure will,' was Devereau's last gasp as Freeman squirrelled for the door.

As the Shire Secretary watched the councillor's gangly frame scurry from his office, a wave of villainy cascaded over his noble existence. 'There's only been one murder in Bowater in the last one hundred years when some sod killed an Irish gold prospector. When it comes to Cr Freeman, I'd like to make it two. There's something going on here,' he thought, as he rose, annoyed, to shut his office door. 'This doesn't make sense. It is usual for officers to attend Council deputations to provide advice when required. The local member will be well aware that his Minister would run rings around any of Bowater's councillors. So, if he is serious about saving the passenger service why would he want to shut me out of the meeting. Maybe that's it. He mightn't be as passionate about saving the service as he claims and can blame the delegation for failing to change the Minister's mind on closure. Perhaps, he simply doesn't want to sully his political stocks by irritating one of the Premier's more accomplished power brokers. The Member for Willaroo, ambition unfulfilled, would see no mileage in sacrificing a chance at ministerial grandeur by giving his Minister any unnecessary angst. They had better know what they are doing or there'll be a train wreck big time,' muttered Devereau with a shake of the head and murder on his mind.

The demise of the swaggie found dead beside the river, gleaned two paragraphs in the *Bugle*. The news item explained that the body was discovered by two youngsters playing among the trees and would be buried in a pauper's grave at two o'clock on Wednesday. Aadje's mother, acutely aware that he was one of the youngsters who found the body, detailed to Aadje the news article and its funeral notice. Aadje, with an unfathomable sense of sorrow and obligation, determined that he would go to the burial even if it meant the four mile walk to the cemetery. He would skip school that day, which in itself had appeal in avoiding his tormentors, and farewell the old swaggie as he deserved.

The Wednesday of the funeral dawned clear, warm and dry. Aadje left home as normal, intending to keep Curlin's Bridge company before making his way to the cemetery. He met Peter as scripted and explained what his intentions were.

'I'd love to come with you Aadje, but it's too far out and

I'd have trouble making it on my legs. I couldn't make it there and back without a ride,' lamented Peter. 'Besides, me mum would kill me if I ducked school.'

'I know,' Aadje sympathised. 'We'll catch up tomorrow.'

The two friends parted. One for school, while the other lay with his head on a battered satchel and searched for solace in the canopy of leaves framing Curlin's Bridge. There he stayed until it was time, by his reckoning, to begin the long trek to the cemetery. He arrived weary, thirsty and dusty and sat on one of the brass plaqued seats dotted throughout God's little acre. Becoming restless with boredom, Aadje turned to the plaque and read aloud,

'Donated by the Balfour family
In memory of Michael, A loving son and brother
Who was tragically taken and passed into Heaven
On May 10, 1946'

A sense of sadness gripped Aadje as he re-read the memorial to a dear departed soul and wondered what the tragedy was.

'They never tell ya,' he reflected in disappointment. The sound of a heavy vehicle on gravel alerted Aadje to the approach of the hearse, followed by another car wearing the wisps of dust thrown up by the black mariah as it made its way to the grave site. Aadje, at distance, followed the sparse funeral entourage to the open burial plot. With the hearse at rest, out jumped two attendants who opened the rear doors and began sliding out the casket, scuffed and chipped. Placing it gently on the ground beside the grave, they waited, like sentinels, on either side of the wooden coffin. The car following sidled up to the hearse and expelled a man of the cloth and a young fellow, snappily dressed in tie and white sport coat and cradling a note book. Aadje, moving as close as he dare, heard the clergyman intoning the love of Jesus, the salvation of the departed and calling on the gates of Heaven to swing open and admit the lonely, the poor and the sinner. The Minister, with eyes cast to the heavens, asked God's forgiveness for the lost soul about to be committed to the ground. Beseeching Almighty God in his infinite wisdom, love and charity to welcome this dearly departed into the Kingdom of Heaven for eternity ever after. Following Psalm 23 and a reading from the scriptures, a hessian bag containing the swaggie's faithful kelpie was dutifully placed atop the casket. The funeral parlour attendants, with the help of the grave digger, then slowly lowered the coffin into its last resting place. The Minister recited a prayer for the soul now lost and, when finished, he, the attendants and the young fellow turned on their heels and scuttled to their cars. The grave digger, meanwhile, began the laborious task of filling the open grave. The last resting place of the old man and his companion would be unmarked and unsullied by history, family and friends. The index of the town's burial records would now be the only stain on his sojourn into oblivion. To the grave the old sundowner took his heritage, his secrets and all loves lost. A sad exit for one of God's forgotten ones.

Aadje staring vacantly at the feverish activity of the grave digger, felt a tinge of grief and tears started to well.

'Hey! Where'd you come from young fella?' The grave digger's gruff voice rang out.

'From town. I wanted to farewell the old swaggie.'

'How'd you get here?' asked the man with the shovel.

'I walked and I'd better get going now.'

'It's four miles back to town. If you grab that shovel over there and give me a hand, I'll give you a lift back home. What's your name son? They call me *Six Foot*,' said a chuckling Arthur McFadden.

Aadje, after giving it some thought, grabbed the shovel and as gently as he could, dropped the heavy clods of dirt onto the slowly submerging coffin and its ornament of hessian.

'Hey, young fella. Put your back into it or we'll be here all day,' smiled the grave digger. With the job finished, Aadje, stealing a last glance at the mound of dirt casting its sombre shadow over the soul of the forgotten, bade the swaggie a heartfelt farewell and climbed into Arthur McFadden's green Bedford for the bumpy ride back into town.

'Where do you live son?' queried the driver.

'Jackson's Road.'

'Well I'll be. So do I. I'll drop you off,' volunteered *Six Foot* McFadden.

Aadje's mum was in her front yard when the truck pulled up. She was surprised and concerned to see him arrive in such circumstances.

'Here's your son, missus. He's a good boy.'

'He'd better be. What's he been doing?' asked Anki in a voice accented in alarm and buffed with Dutch brogue.

The grave digger narrated the afternoon's events to a mother who understood her son's need to show his respects to the old man and thanked the driver for bringing him home. She was not angry that he wagged school to attend the swaggie's funeral. She grasped Aadje's need in that regard, but was hurt that he had not let her in on his little secret.

Some days after the sundowner's committal Devereau, found himself sitting in his plush leather chair to the right hand of Cr Dixon as the Shire President welcomed councillors and staff to the October meeting of Council. Agenda in place and Minutes of the previous meeting confirmed, the conclave moved to the substantive matters for consideration. The usual roads, garbage, footpaths and minor works occupied their share of the agenda. At the appropriate time, Cr Freeman moved to resolve that a delegation of three councillors be elected to meet with the Minister for Transport and the local member at Parliament House to argue Bowater's case for retaining the VR passenger service to Melbourne. The resolution charged the Shire Secretary with responsibility for cataloguing a comprehensive justification for the service's continuation. Freeman stressed the local member's advice that only councillors should be part of the delegation and that success would be more assured in the absence of Council officers. Devereau expressed his dissent from the local member's strictures in the same terms he had enunciated earlier to Cr Freeman. It was to no avail. As Shire

Secretary he was excluded from the delegation by seven votes to two. With a dismissive shrug of his shoulders, he observed Council elect Crs Freeman, Ferguson and Shire President Dixon to make the presentation to the Minister. Devereau was assigned the task of communicating Council's decision to the local member at the earliest opportunity.

The issue that jangled his nerve and resolve the most was that related to the Engineer's report on lifting the height of the weir. Andy Dawson tabled his report and argued strongly that the matter be referred to committee for a thorough analysis of the impact on the river and adjoining properties should the level of the weir be raised. Devereau supported his Engineer in his call to refer it to committee and waited with baited breath for the inevitable resolution from the gang of six overriding the Engineer's advice. The silence was manifest. Crs Owen and McNichol threw daggers of animosity across the Council chamber with some of their number keeping a wary eye on Devereau's reaction. Seizing the moment, Cr Keegan moved that Council resolve to refer the matter to committee. A proposition quickly seconded by Cr Clark. At which point and before any vote could be taken, Crs Curlin and McNichol scurried from the chamber. Thereby, going some way to protecting their credibility with a friend who expected that they, for old time's sake, would look after a mate and save his precious beach on the river. They could now look Steve Adair in the eye and cynically claim no ownership in burying the issue in committee. Following Keegan's brief statement in support of the Engineer's advice, a show of hands, some raised more slowly than others, saw the motion and the matter of the weir pass into the bowels of committee. The Chair, having considered the agenda, and there being no other business declared the meeting closed at 9:20 p.m. As councillors in unison, shuffled their papers and mumbled to each other, Devereau slid back his chair, snatched up his papers and made his way out of the Council chamber. Walking into the foyer to return his papers to his office, Cr McNichol brushed past, stopped, and with a steely glare of unresolved anger said with acrimony and delicious irony, 'we owe you Bill. There's a lot of water to pass under the bridge yet, and we have long memories.'

'So be it,' was Devereau's less than confident response. 'It was the right decision councillor. To do otherwise would have been a travesty. Now, if you'll excuse me, I must be off.' With that Devereau, having dispatched his sheaths of burden to his office, began the short stroll home to the comfort of his darling wife. Devereau enjoyed the walk home after Council. It gave him space to clear his mind and reflect on the events of the night. This night he welcomed the loneliness of his own company. While flushed with success, he knew that he had let slip the dogs of war and he harboured lingering concern for his longevity as Shire Secretary.

'Ah, well! We'll see what tomorrow brings,' were his thoughts as he opened his front door and disappeared inside to the warmth of a loving wife and son.

CHAPTER EIGHT

Into the Void

Bill Devereau, at his desk tending to the daily demands of the Shire and its residents, called out for Millie. Millie, face silhouetted by morning shards of sunlight, poked her coiffed head around the door and asked. 'Yes Bill, how can I help?'

'Would you mind getting in touch with the local member of Parliament's office and arranging for me to meet with him over the delegation to the Minister. Parliament's not sitting, so we should be able to catch up with him pretty soon. I want to sort out the timing of a delegation so I can organise and brief the councillors attending,' requested Devereau cheerily.

In some ways he was quietly relieved that Council chose to exclude him from the delegation, where failure could well be sheeted home to him. But, in his more reflective moments he feared for their capacity to negotiate a successful outcome. His father's oft repeated, *'you can't put brains in monuments,'* came back to haunt him each time he pondered the fabric of the delegation as ratified by Council. Returning to the task at hand, his solitude was broken by the figure of his Engineer standing in front of him. Devereau, pen in hand, looked up and with raised eyebrows asked. 'What's happening Andy?'

Andrew Dawson, wearing a grin of sublime satisfaction expressed his complete surprise at last night's weir vote and wondered what was behind the collapse in support for raising its level.

'Did you have a hand in the vote Bill? Dawson asked. 'You copped a few glares during the meeting.'

'Let's just say Andy, that when push comes to shove, a little leverage goes a hell of a long way.'

'I don't know how you did it, but whatever it was worked a treat. It was a most pleasing decision and, for a change, the right one. Fairness has prevailed.'

'Keep in mind Andy, it has only been buried. It hasn't gone away and they'll try again whenever they think the time is right.'

'Yeah, I understand that Bill. But, as executive officer of the Public Works committee, I'll make sure it stays buried indefinitely,' came the Engineer's determined response.

'Do your best Andy, but remember to keep a watch on 'em. They're crafty and while I've been able to mould their hearts and minds to the common good this time, they'll try again.' With that the Engineer, still sporting the grin of a victor, left Devereau's office as quietly as he had entered.

Millie's dulcet tone interrupted his concentration and detailed that the local member could meet with him at two o'clock today in his electorate office in the main street.

'That was quick Millie. Well done, you're a gem.'

With new found gusto, Devereau set about readying himself for his meeting with the local member. Country Party stalwart, Anthony Heyfield had represented the seat of Willaroo since 1947. His ascendency to parliament's lofty perch came earlier than he expected when the Cain minority government was forced to the polls by a conservative Legislative Council using its numbers to block supply. Paving the way for the Liberal/Country Party to grab power and elevating Heyfield to the sanctity of Spring Street and the temple of the righteous. Heyfield had been elected on the back of his Party allegiance, war service and charm. With the recent election of the Bolte government, he had expected to be rewarded with a Ministry as a long serving and loyal Party member. He had increased his majority in each of the elections he had contested and felt slighted when over looked by a Premier whose Ministerial largesse appeared to run out south of the Great Dividing Range. Or, so it seemed to Heyfield. The proposed Council delegation gave him an opportunity to further enhance his credentials with the Minister and demonstrate his political skills and loyalty.

Sometime later, as he was leaving his office to meet Heyfield, he called out to Millie to let her know he was off, and that he would be a little longer as he would call in for a haircut on the way back. Millie, with a smile that lit up her eyes, cautioned her boss. 'Be careful, Mr Devereau. They don't call him *Short Back'n Ears* for nothing.' Gilbert Young, an ex-army barber, was exposed as an alcoholic when he began to snip ears with the same dexterity, he clipped hair. Many a local had experienced the sting of an earlobe nicked in honour of sartorial elegance. As the only barber in town, Bertie held sway. While none dared to ask for a shave, the men of the district had little choice when it came to a short back and sides. Only then did they find real fear in the alcohol-fuelled breath of a barber grappling with his scissors.

Devereau's meeting with the Member for Willaroo was pleasant, as it was brief. Heyfield promised to contact the Minister for Transport's office and arrange for a meeting at the earliest opportunity.

'This issue is of great significance to my electorate and I want to make sure that the outcome is to the satisfaction of my constituency. Rest assured Bill, I don't want the passenger service closed any more than Council does.' Devereau articulated the value of the service to the elderly, the young and those without private transport and stressed the dire consequences for the town if the service be discontinued.

'The issue for the Minister, Bill, is the cost effectiveness of the service. The passenger train runs at a loss and that makes arguments for its retention problematic. But Council's delegation and I will do our best to convince the Minister that the town needs the service. Of course, it's not just Bowater that's affected. It would impact on every town down the line. My problem is, most of them are in my electorate.'

Devereau stood to take his leave and winced at the gauze concealing the Member's left earlobe.

'Thanks for your time Anthony. You'll let Millie know the arrangements when you find out?' asserted Devereau.

'Parliament resumes next week. I'll try for some time during that week,' reflected Heyfield, gingerly fingering his earlobe.

Devereau, on returning to his office and unscathed by his visit to the barber, let Millie know that the member's office would contact her regarding the meeting with the Minister.

'When we know the date,' he told Millie, 'we'll organise some train tickets for the delegation'

'I see you got out of *Short Back'n Ears* in one piece,' said Millie with a smile.

'I did indeed Millie. Although, I'm not sure that the local member did,' responded Devereau with a laugh. 'You'd reckon he'd get his hair cut in Melbourne where it'd be safer, wouldn't you? Oh, well, you know what they say about brains and monuments.' With that, Devereau left his office for the evening. For tonight, and before wending his way home for supper, he would have a few beers to celebrate having survived, for the third time, the manic scissors wielded by the local barber who finesses his skill and euphoria in an ocean of whisky.

Peter and Aadje entered the school gates as per routine. Early November saw the warmth of late spring roll across the landscape. Blackie and his disciples, as usual, greeted Aadje with their traditional welcome. Jeers and derision that reflected on Aadje's heritage, physical features and social status assailed him as he made his way to the lockers.

This time though, things did not go as planned for Blackie and his knaves. A thunderous voice, propelled with jets of anger, boomed, 'Jerome Gavin. You get here to me. And bring your layabout friends with you,' ranted Mr Rae. Mr Rae, an imposing figure of a man, brooked no defiance. As Blackie's wood work teacher, he had grasped the nettle that gave Blackie Gavin his sting and was about to crush it, roots and all. Before a sheepish Blackie and startled Aadje, Mr Rae, with a finger the size of a sausage, jabbed Jerome Gavin in the chest and, in a guttural turn of phrase delivered through gritted teeth, reminded the callow youth in front of him of his proper station in life. 'Gavin, I've had enough of your smart aleck behaviour.

You've been tormenting that kid for far too long and it's going to stop right now. You and your mates have become too big for your boots and you need a good foot in the behind.'

'We didn't mean it sir,' was Blackie's pitiful cry for leniency, if not understanding. Mr Rae, having none of it, with a finger stabbing away at Blackie's shaking chest he raised his voice a number of octaves to a bellow.

'Don't you dare interrupt me you little upstart. I don't care who your father is, but if I catch you or these reprobates teasing that young fellow again, not only will I tell your old man, I'll come after you. I can assure you Jerome, you won't like that. Now get yourselves to class and don't cross me again,' Mr Rae's parting threat sent Blackie and his chastened cohort scuttling off to the safety of their classroom.

Peter and Aadje, taken aback by Mr Rae's tirade, felt the

tremor of relief that comes when a bully meets his match. Peter, barely disguising a smile, whispered conspiratorially to Aadje. 'Did you catch Blackie's real name Aadje? Jerome. Do you believe that? Next time he has a go at us, we'll call him Jerome. That'll fix him.'

'It would just make him madder. Anyway, I'll show 'em. They'll sit up and take notice when I dive off the bridge. Then they'll see I'm as good as they are,' added Aadje as they ascended the steps to their lockers.

November 11, Remembrance Day, witnessed the usual dignitaries, returned servicemen and town folk attend the memorial service in honour of the fallen. A time that always elicits a tinge of guilt in Devereau, whose reserved occupation status kept him from the ravages of war and safely cocooned on the home front. The march of the ANZAC's down Fossicker Street, the traditional minute's silence at 11:00 o'clock and keynote speech were greeted by the warmth of a sun in search of its zenith. At the conclusion of ceremonies, the returned servicemen and fellow travellers stampeded for one of Bowater's four pubs to swim in a sea of amber, play some *two-up* and relive the past forged on the field of battle. Devereau joined the revellers for a beer or two and accepted the accolades of the joyous for Council's part in the organisation of the day. Devereau had spent time with the RSL sub-Branch executive planning and coordinating the Remembrance Day service. With a number of ex-servicemen gracing Council's sacred portals, both councillors and staff, it was an easy and pleasant task to manage the Council's involvement in the day.

Cr Freeman swanned into Devereau's office right on cue. 'Thanks for coming at such short notice councillor. I let Cr Dixon know yesterday about your meeting with the Minister. As you are probably aware, it is scheduled for one o'clock on the 14th in his Spring Street office. He'll meet you during the luncheon adjournment of the House. I'll have Millie arrange some train tickets for you, Cr Ferguson and Shire President Dixon. The train gets in at 11:30 so you've got a good hour to get from Spencer Street to Parliament House.'

'Oh! That won't be necessary Bill. Cyril caught up with me and Cr Ferguson last night and wants to drive. When he spoke to you yesterday, he forgot about a commitment he made to the CWA to address their next get together. Unfortunately, the dates clash. He's gotta be back for their meeting at seven o'clock and if he goes by train he won't be back in Bowater until nearer eight o'clock,' explained Freeman.

'You're kiddin' me,' exclaimed an incredulous Devereau. 'You're going to Melbourne to argue the case for retaining the train service, and you're going by car. It's not a good look councillor.'

'It'll be alright. The Minister doesn't need to know we came to the big smoke by car. We'll tell him we arrived by train,' grunted Freeman, with barely camouflaged annoyance. 'It's a pity Cyril couldn't be here. As far as I know he's having his header serviced for the coming harvest. Otherwise he'd be here to explain for himself,' was all that Freeman could offer.

'If that's the way you want it, I'm in no position to argue. But I wish you would reconsider. I know the train doesn't leave 'till nine in the morning and doesn't get back in much before eight in the evening, but, just once, it might be worth the inconvenience,' cautioned Devereau, floored senseless by what he'd just heard. A caution lost on Cr Freeman who repeated the Shire President's wish to go by car so that he could make his scheduled meeting and not let down the ladies in the CWA.

'Okay then. You have the date and the time. I'll leave it up to you as to how you get there. Though, I urge you to think about it, councillor.'

'You worry too much Bill. Cr Ferguson has offered to drive and we'll park out of sight. We know what we're doing. Besides, Heyfield's on our side,' came Freeman's parting shot as he left Devereau's office. Rising to close his office door and shaking his head with bewildered foreboding, Devereau called out to Millie and asked her to forget the railway tickets he had asked her to organise. 'Silly bugger. I get paid to worry,' were his last thoughts as he resumed his seat behind a desk now lacquered by the broad brush of misgiving.

Aadje turned fifteen on November 13 and his mother had invited Peter around for afternoon tea to help celebrate the occasion. Mrs Devereau baked a cake and took a canister of milk to Jackson's Road. Peter, with his dad's financial help, had bought Aadje a model Bedford truck and was looking forward to seeing the surprise on his face as he opened his gift. While the two mothers nattered about all-things family, the boys enjoyed their milk and cake and then went rabbiting. 'Don't be too long,' chorused the mothers, as the boys, ferret cage in tow, made their way out the front door and into the street. With the two women warming to the company of each other, time passed quickly.

As the afternoon shadows lengthened towards sunset, Aadje and Peter, excited beyond comprehension, burst in with the lifeless form of a rabbit as a trophy to their success. Dispatched deftly with a skill taught by his father, Aadje had brought home a prize for his mother to make many an evening meal. Mrs Devereau, recoiling from the limp image of the recently deceased, decided it was time to begin the walk back to the Devereau home on the other side of the river. After Peter thanked Mrs Kuiper for inviting him to Aadje's birthday celebration, he and his mother took their leave, with Alice Devereau saying that they must get together again sometime soon. Anki stood at the garden gate, arm around her now fifteen-year-old son, and thanked them for the cake and milk as she bid them farewell with a wave.

November 15 began as any other day. Devereau arrived at his office promptly at 8:30, said good morning to his clerk, serious in disposition, guarding the entrance to the cavern of his discontent and to his faithful Millie, before attacking the papers neatly stacked on his desk. Looking sheepish, if not a little crestfallen, Cr Dixon appeared at his office door and, without a word, projected himself into the room. Devereau, full of expectation, looked up and asked how the meeting with the Minister went?

'Did you swing the day councillor?' eyed Devereau, his excitement building. Dixon gave Devereau a look so vacant that he thought his Shire President had suffered a serious malady. Dixon, wringing his hat in clenched fists and staring at the floor stuttered, in a voice barely audible. 'Not good. Not good at all.'

'What do you mean, not good? You explained the need for the passenger service, didn't you?'

'Well, we tried,' was all that Devereau could extract from a man clearly absorbed by despair and the failure of hindsight.

'Don't tell me we're going to lose the train. What the hell happened? I thought Heyfield was on our side,' Devereau spat out in frustration and foreboding.

'When we entered his office, big too it was, and while his secretary was making us tea, he asked us where we'd parked the car. It was a cunning ambush, but at the time we weren't thinking and fell for it. Cr Ferguson instinctively told him he'd parked his car behind Parliament House in the shade of the elm trees.'

'Oh! Great,' interjected a now despondent Shire Secretary. 'Go on.'

'The Minister said the meeting would be pretty short because he didn't want to delay us leaving for home any longer than necessary. He asked us about the need for a passenger service, given that it's costly to run and patronage has fallen.' At which point Devereau grimaced in expectation. 'He finished the meeting after fifteen minutes and told us he would be recommending to cabinet that the service, based on cost and patronage, be terminated. His parting shot was the dagger in the back Bill. He just smiled and told us that, while the freight service will stay, it was very clear, given we drove to Melbourne to meet with him, the passenger service was an expensive indulgence us and his government obviously didn't need. He thanked us for coming and ushered us out of his office with the instruction to drive safely.'

Devereau sat gazing at the ceiling in silent tribute to a man who metaphorically twisted the knife, and orchestrated the fate of the passenger service in one artful and deft slap of Ministerial cunning.

'Having put your foot in it, did you try to explain that you had to drive because the train's scheduled travel timetable is inconvenient and the level of service needs to be increased with more trains, not less?' Devereau questioned, rattling with censure and misgiving.

'We never got that far Bill. The Minister was a closed book as soon as he knew we had driven to the big smoke.'

'I did warn Cr Freeman of the risks you were taking and I was assured all would be well. Now we've got real problems.'

'I know Bill. It's all my doing and I'll have to wear what comes.'

'Where's Heyfield stand in all this?' queried Devereau.

'When we left the Minister's office, Anthony said he'd talk to the Minister. Heyfield says he's a mate of his and he might be able to swing it for us.'

'I wouldn't bet on it, Cyril. But we'll see what happens.

Who's making the report to the next Council meeting? It will need to be a good one,' finished Devereau, nailing culpability to the masthead of arrogance.

'Cr Freeman, who pushed for the delegation, wanted to give the report so as, I guess, he could bask in the limelight of success. Given what's happened, I reckon he'll run for the hills. As Shire President, it will, for good or bad, fall on me to make the report.' As Cr Dixon got up to leave, his hat eschewed from its pummelling, Devereau instructed with all the authority he could muster, 'choose your words carefully, if you know what I mean?'

'Don't worry Bill. I will,' were the last words Devereau heard as his Shire President disappeared into the foyer and the crisis of his own making.

Devereau, once more alone, put his head in his hands and, with exasperation writ large, said to an empty room and quoted from his favourite bard. '*It is but a dark comedy where the common curse of mankind – folly and ignorance is crowned with failure.*' Devereau, in the hope of salvaging something from the disaster, made a note to catch up with the local member and called for his Engineer to brief him on the drama and warn him of the impending community backlash.

'Some councillors only deviate into common sense when they've exhausted every other alternative,' thought Devereau as he closed his folder and awaited the arrival of Andy Dawson. Following Devereau's description of the meeting with the Minister, best described as a debacle, Andy Dawson equally as incredulous as his boss, shook his head in resigned disbelief.

'What do you reckon we should do next Bill?'

'I'll catch up with Heyfield before the November Council meeting and see what he's got to say. But, until then, we'll just have to await developments, or Ministerial announcements,' lamented Devereau.

'Oh, well. We'll leave it then and see what happens,' Dawson remarked as he made his way out of the office, closing the Shire Secretary's door quietly behind him.

Oblivious to the nuances of local government, Peter and Aadje, presented with the pleasures that come with the warming glow of the November sun, continued their roaming along the banks of the Daraleet and around the town's precincts. Spring was transitioning into summer as the district warmed up for its seasonal bake. Hot days and clear, balmy nights were moving into a landscape preparing for the summer harvest. Aadje and Peter often spent time with Mr Kwong who, with a smile and a bow, amused them by venerating Confucius and his infinite wisdom. Leaving his company, laden with the fruits of his labour, the boys would wander off home to present their mothers with Mr Kwong's bounteous gifts. During their travels, Aadje would occasionally strip off and have a paddle in some secluded spot along the river. All the while, Peter would watch with pangs of envy, tinged with concern for his friend lest he get into trouble in a river so inviting. For as Peter knew, Aadje was not a good swimmer and that he, Peter, was useless to him should the river's embrace turn sinister. Between school and Aadje running washing around town for his mother, the boys explored the broad undercurrent that was Bowater. They went rabbiting together, a slow process with Peter struggling to keep abreast of Aadje's exuberant pursuit of meat for his mother's table. From the sanctity of the river's bushy, tree shrouded bank, the boys conspiratorially watched the arrival of the recently departed at the aging shed that masqueraded as a funeral parlour and occupied their days by meandering, wherever whim took them, in the company of each other. Lazy days spent amusing each other with their hopes and dreams.

'I'm gonna be a truck driver. I want to see the world. It'll be just me and me truck. Nobody'll be able to push me around. Blackie will be nowhere to be seen and I can give some money to my mum. That would be good, wouldn't it Peter?' Aadje dreamed.

'Yeah. It'd be good,' Peter responded.

'What do you wanna do when you leave school Pete?'

'I don't know. With me legs, I guess I'll need to get a job in a bank or something. I could work behind a desk like dad does. I dunno,' was all Peter could offer. 'I wouldn't mind working for a newspaper like the *Bugle* I guess,' mumbled Peter when struck with an afterthought of enlightenment. The days passed like that. They would sit for long periods of time and watch the trucks come and go from the cannery, with Aadje detailing for Peter the make and model of each truck as it disgorged its cargo into the bowels of rural reality and of an industry, like Peter's crutches, a prop to local prosperity. When coupled with the cooperative milk factory, the two business icons of the town provided much of the employment opportunities for the landless, the dispossessed and the battler. They were the steam engines for a town driven by the rural idyll, where opportunity is cleft with inequality. So were Peter and Aadje's days. Soul mates wandering wherever inclination took them, searching for acceptance, solitude and a future with their dreams fulfilled.

November's Shire Council meeting dawned as scheduled. The Chair gave his report on the outcome of Council's delegation to the Minister and was met by an audience muted by a stunned and stony silence. Dixon, neglecting to mention the Minister's repartee on how they arrived, glossed over the calamity by stressing that the meeting was, in any case, a waste of time because the Minister had already made up his mind. He concluded his report with a dig at the local member who, he claimed, was less than helpful when support was most needed. By inference, the Shire President, with cunning aforethought, sheeted home the failure of the delegation to the front door of Heyfield's office and blamed a belligerent government for the demise of the passenger service. The cadet journalist, the whites of his eyes a beacon of zeal, scribbled as fast as he could to capture every word Dixon spat out. This, Devereau mused, could well be the banner headline in the next edition of the *Bugle*. '*Passenger Service Derailed. Council Blames Government and Calls on Local Member to do more.*' Following the Chair's report, and amidst the grumbles of angst circulating around the chamber, Devereau advised Council that he had met with the Member for Willaroo and Heyfield had indicated that the decision to dismantle the passenger service was not reversible. The Member stressed that he had lobbied the Minister to shelve the decision, but to no avail. However, the service will not terminate immediately, but will be phased out over the next twelve months and will cease altogether at the end of 1956. The current five-day service will drop to three days in January, then to two by mid-year and stop completely in December next year. The freight service, Devereau reported, is to be retained as it currently operates. Following the reports, councillors expressed levels of disappointment tempered by the availability of private transport to their respective constituents. Crs Keegan and Clark, whose voter base was less endowed and relied more on the train service, stridently opposed the decision and, with barbs veiled in mockery, made much of Dixon's discomfort and the silence of his fellow delegates. Council heard that the new tip was on target to open in December and that the old landfill was all but capped. Devereau presented his proposal to replace Curlin's Bridge, with the Engineer tabling some design briefs, projected costs and suggested construction time frame. The Engineer reiterated that the one lane timber bridge was not meeting Bowater's growing traffic needs and was frustrating trucking activity, east and west. Particularly, those transports accessing the freight yards from the east. The aging timber bridge, he reported, was becoming costly to repair and maintain. Dawson stressed that the new bridge design would make it harder for the young bucks to dive off its apex each summer. They, unfortunately, see it as their civic duty to climb atop its railings and join the long list of heroes by jumping into immortality. Devereau, with Dawson's support, confirmed that the reconstruction of the town's main street shopping centre would begin early next year, with completion expected in the latter half of 1956. The meeting ended with the cadet journalist scrambling for the Shire President to add more fuel to the flame for his upcoming story on the demise of the town's passenger service. The zealous pursuit of a good story is a career defining moment for any young journalist on the make. Michael O'Hara, just one year into his cadetship, smelled personal glory in this story and sure beats reporting on a swaggie's burial in a pauper's grave. Bailing Dixon up against the bar table, preventing any escape, the young reporter pumped his target with all manner of questions, without once asking how the delegation made their way to Melbourne. It would be a story well told as the *Bugle* hit the streets in the weeks ahead.

December descended with its signature blazing sun and shimmering heat haze that distorted a landscape struggling against the onslaught. Harvest was in full overload. Grain trucks driven with missionary passion, rumbled in and out of the concrete wheat silos whose towering shadows kept the railway siding company. Aadje and Peter, bedecked in shorts and singlets, made merry while the sun did shine. Snakes, the odd goanna and the regulation array of frill-necked lizards and shinglebacks added spice to their meanderings, and often gained their undivided attention whenever strolling along the river bank. Aadje introduced Peter to a new sport, where, high on adrenalin fuelled guilt, they would lay hidden by the drooping foliage of the weeping willows and spy on the nuns and trainee priests frolicking in the cooling waters of their calling. From the opposite side of the river, Peter and Aadje could, undetected, observe the spiritual joy of young people communing with their God and free of the strictures and moral code of their order. The seminary, imposing in its three-storey grandeur, stared down, disapproving, casting barbs of sin at the revellers temporarily basking in freedom's divine glory. Aadje's Christmas was, as it had been for the past three years, a lonely time where he and his mother made do with whatever her paltry earnings could lay upon the table. She did her best to assuage his feelings of abandonment, the loss of his dad and the joy that Christmas presents bring. At this time of year, Aadje found more comfort with his ferrets than reminders of tragedy and grief of Christmas past. Peter's yuletide witnessed the trappings of a family privileged with the capacity to laden a table with the fare traditional for this spiritual time of year. For Peter, who was turning fourteen in March, Christmas presented as an opportunity to spend time with his father who would regale him of his boyhood days of mischief and fun around the back streets of Footscray. This particular Christmas would become carved in Peter's memory, for his father, with uncharacteristic excitement, invited Peter to follow him to the back shed. On swinging open the weathered door, his father looked at him and said, 'what do you think Peter?' There, beside the Ford, in all its Indian glory, sat a 1939 Scout with sidecar attached. It squatted, coiled for action, in all its gleaming red livery with its gold embossed Indian war bonnet emblazoned across the tank. Its cracked leather seat and blackened exhaust spoke of history, freedom and roads well-travelled. Devereau, coveting the moment as much as his motorcycle, repeated for Peter, 'What do you think?'

'It's a beauty dad. When did you get it?'

'I picked it up yesterday. Your mum's not too keen on it, but I just loved it the minute I spotted it in Mr Pringle's garage when I was last there with the car. Got it for a good price and I'll take it for a spin in the next day or two. Your mother refuses to be seen dead in the sidecar,' rambled Devereau, a quiver of anticipation doing its best to temper his excitement. Devereau circumnavigated his purchase a number of times and, during each orbit, would stop and gently fondle and stroke various parts of its iron headed beauty. On hearing Mrs Devereau's rhythmic call for lunch, Devereau, with one last look at his prized possessions, shut the door. Leaving the darkness to embrace his beloved, he slowly followed Peter inside for the warmth of a Christmas lunch with family.

As January farewelled December, it couriered in a landscape baked dry by the relentless glare of a fiery sun that wearied the land into submission. The hot northerlies, when migrating south, sapped the energy from all living things. It was a stubborn heat that wilted the bush and drove fauna to cooling refuges of their own choosing and the locals to water. Summer twilight once more witnessed the young bucks of the town re-join their sport with Sgt O'Reilly as they, at every chance, tested their resolve and courage by diving off Curlin's Bridge. With their *cockatoos* strategically ensconced as look outs, they would wait for the all clear and leap into the cool embrace of the river below. There to surface with a pride swelled by the cheers of onlookers awaiting their turn to triumph. Aadje, who watched their antics while camouflaged among the dappled shadows dancing along the river's tree lined banks, steeled himself for the day that he would take the leap and show his tormentors that he was as good as they. He would show them because his quest was his salvation. He would be redeemed as one of them. It was the middle of January when Aadje whispered conspiratorially to Peter.

'I'm gonna do the bridge this arvo', Aadje pledged. Peter, becoming excited with a mix of expectation and apprehension, allowed Aadje to detail his plans and was easily cajoled into being Aadje's *cockatoo* for his leap. At the anointed time, later in the afternoon, with the summer breeze caressing his bare skin, Aadje readied himself to do the deed. Peter, stationed on the narrow walk way to the entrance to the bridge, yelled to Aadje that nothing was coming and it was all clear. On cue, Aadje Kuiper deftly hoisted his spindly frame onto the top railing of Curlin's Bridge. He teetered on the balls of his bare feet and fought for balance while scanning the murky depths some thirty odd feet below. The sun, settling lower on the horizon, threw fingers of shadow over the single span bridge and a reddish ambience silhouetted the pale figure perched high above the river. The still and quiet of the January twilight was broken only by the echoing screech of galahs winging their way to asylum in the river gums and willows that stood guard along its banks. Aadje, steadier now, arms limp beside the twitching sinews of his thighs, felt the sharp cramp of strain and fear grip his all too thin body and take a stranglehold on his spirit. Beads of perspiration formed on his young brow, his blue eyes, vacant and unblinking, stared at the drifting water far below. His blond, unkempt, hair wisped over his large ears and droplets of sweat trickled down his colourless cheeks and hung, glistening from his jaw. The waters of the Daraleet, gouged by the wash of centuries between canyon walls of clay, danced a glitter as shafts of muted light flickered through the leaves of the trees escorting its progress. The river, cloaked in its summer twilight livery was passive and serene. Aadje, his brain crowded with fear, wrestled with his courage and willed his body to jump. But fright would not release its hold and kept him chained by invisible links more powerful than any forged steel. Locked in a struggle with the unseen demons of anxiety, Aadje took a deep breath, closed his eyes tight, raised his arms and with a violent blast of his own will power broke the shackles of cowardice and launched into space. Suspended like a marionette on thermal strings, Aadje's slender frame hung momentarily, then, gathering speed plunged toward the shadowed water below.

Aadje, arms flailing and legs askew, fractured the soul of the Daraleet River without fanfare and very little grace. The explosion of flesh on water echoed along the canyons of gums and startled the resting galahs and cockatoos from their perches in a cacophony that briefly shattered the twilight tranquillity. Aadje Kuiper disappeared into a foaming cauldron that thumped a spray of water some five feet into the air. And within seconds, silence once more descended upon the river. The Daraleet, disturbed from its slumber, had snatched Aadje to its bosom and stroked him with cool and comforting tenderness. All that remained of Adje's leap was the concentric waves rippling from its epicentre. The point of impact where youthful frailty met nature's embracing arms and the circles of perfect symmetry, like fading dreams, disappeared from whence they come.

Peter, having moved to the top of the parapet, watched the ripples ebb away in awe and anticipation. An eerie silence descended over the river while Peter waited for his friend to break the water and reveal his crown of glory to the world. Growing anxious at the delay, Peter leaned over the railing and stared at the muddied water below, waiting for Aadje to break the surface and claim his rightful place in the annals of Bowater's youth as a self-fulfilled legend. With fear's icy tentacles invading his sensitivities, he called out to Aadje'. 'Where are you? You're not funny. Get out of the water, you're scaring me. Get out.' Receiving no answer, agitation making way for panic, Peter, in despair and waving his crutches, began screaming for help. With tears streaming down his cheeks, he frantically waved to a flatbed truck making its way slowly over the bridge. Having stopped, the driver poked his head from the open window and asked. 'What's up kid?'

'It's my friend Aadje. He dived off the bridge and hasn't come up. I don't know where he's gone,' a clearly distressed Peter Devereau blubbered out.

'Oh! Jesus,' the driver groaned as he swung open the door of his truck and in long strides bounded from the bridge, down the bank and, minus his boots, but still clothed, dived into the flowing waters of the river. Peter watched from the crest of the bridge while his good samaritan ducked and surfaced many a time, broadening his search with each dive. Peter, tears mingling with the sweat cascading down his face, shook and wrung his hands, despair growing each time the truck driver broke the surface for air. When all seemed lost, the river released its captives and, with an explosion of cascading water, the driver propelled Aadje to the surface of the river and began dragging his still form to its muddied fringe.

'You found him. Is he alright?' Peter yelled as he stumbled his way from the bridge to join his friend on the bank. On reaching Aadje's prone, limp body, Peter dropped his crutches and begged his friend to get up. 'Stop foolin' around Aadje. You've scared me enough. Why won't you get up? This is not funny,' babbled Peter, overwhelmed by dread and foreboding.

The truck driver sitting, heaving with his effort, looked at Peter and, through shortened breath and with as gentle a voice as he could muster said. 'It'll be alright son. Why don't you go and have a little rest by that tree over there? I'll take care of your friend.' Distressed and in a state of shock, Peter did as he was bid and shuffled away to keep his own company. The driver, kneeling beside Aadje's lifeless form, slowly shook his head as harsh reality told him that the lad was gone. Having recognised the inert body before him as the young fellow who helped him bury the old swaggie and wrought with growing pangs of grief, he cast his eyes into the soul of the river and cursed its very waters as the work of the devil.

The truck, door ajar, had blocked the bridge and travellers began gathering at the bridge's railing. Spotting the grave digger and the prone figure of a lad on the river bank below, they asked if he needed help. 'Get O'Reilly and we'll need an ambulance. Quick,' instructed the grave digger, anxiety shrilling his tone. Realising the seriousness and urgency of the circumstances, some hurried off to carry out the truck driver's bidding. Peter, on catching the urgency, burst into a fresh flurry of tears and became inconsolable when he saw the grave digger remove his shirt and gently lay it over Aadje's still and waxen form. Rivulets of water drifted aimlessly down Aadje's lifeless arms and tufts of sodden hair poked their way out from under his makeshift shroud of death. Looking over to Peter, now shaking uncontrollably, he asked, 'who's your father and where can we find him?' Barely able to speak, Peter somehow got out his father was William Devereau and that he worked at the Council. With a tinge of relief, Arthur McFadden, in realising who his father was, looked at the gathering faces on the bridge and yelled. 'Can someone get Bill Devereau down here? His kid's in a bad way and he needs him. He lives in River Road.' Two faces disappeared from view and, with the speed of Adonis, sprinted for the Devereau residence. Meanwhile, two other onlookers had scrambled down the bank and, standing before Aadje's still and shrouded form, one of them asked. 'Are you okay Arthur? You don't look too good.'

'I've seen better days, Bugsy,' he responded with a grimace. Fighting back tears, he asked Bugsy and the bloke with him to check on the boy rocking backwards and forwards under his tree of anguish. 'I've called for his father, but take care of him will you until he gets here.' Bugsy, with a hint of concern, looked to Peter and scrambled off with his ally to offer comfort to the kid. David, *Bugsy*, Moran found fame, but not fortune as Bowater's beefy full back, when, during one game, he tried to drown the opposition's full forward in the ankle-deep mud that covered the goal square. Seething with white hot rage, Bugsy had to be restrained by the umpires and half his team mates lest he do the hapless forward an injury, or worse. He escaped sanction at the League's tribunal because the umpire had no idea with what to charge him. They found no rule in the League's constitution that covered attempted murder. From there Bugsy Moran became a hero to a legion of young footballers everywhere.

Sgt O'Reilly, having arrived breathless with Constable Allison, knelt down beside Aadje and on folding back his temporary shroud, sighed and silently pronounced him dead.

'What happened, Arthur?'

'Just like the other youngsters, he dived off the bridge. Only he didn't come up. It was sheer luck I managed to find him.'

'Who's that lad with Bugsy?' questioned the Sergeant.

'It's his mate. He's Devereau's kid. They've gone to get him,' responded Arthur, in a voice quieted by sorrow and laced with regret.

'Oh! Christ. What a bloody mess?' was all O'Reilly could extol as his mind's eye visualised the required investigation and reports. 'Will these kids never learn?' lamented a sergeant whose frustration loomed as large as his ample girth.

'Come on Bill. We've all done it. We've just been damn lucky. This kid's luck just ran out. You know he helped me bury the sundowner a little way back and I gave him a lift home in me truck. He wanted to be a truckie, you know. He has a nice mum and he looked like a good kid,' eulogised McFadden.

Bill Devereau, arriving in a state of breathless agitation, and, on seeing the lifeless, covered, body of Aadje Kuiper on the ground, feared the worst. Stumbling down the bank, a wave of relief descended upon him as he realised that the two good legs of the dead youth before him were not those of his son. Having got the message that his son was in a bad way, he barged through his front gate without even calling to his wife, and headed directly to Curlin's Bridge. On spotting his son being consoled by a couple of good-hearted locals, Devereau sprinted to Peter's side and wrapped him in both arms. Peter sobbed uncontrollably on his father's shoulder who kept repeating. 'It's alright, Peter. I'm here now.' Peter, through a veil of tears buried his head in his father's comfort, babbled. 'It's my fault. I couldn't help him. I'm a cripple dad and I let him down.' Devereau, with tears forming, cringed and hugged his son even tighter.

'It's not your fault. Nobody could have helped Aadje. It has nothing to do with your legs. It was his time,' was all that Devereau could say as his son's distress reverberated along the river's bank and was lost among the trees, the passive spectators of the tragedy unfolding. 'Come on son, I'll take you home.' Cradling Peter in his arms, Devereau, on passing O'Reilly, asked if the sergeant needed anything.

'I'll need to talk to your boy at some stage,' said the sergeant, his voice riddled with sympathy. 'But I'll wait until you tell me it is okay.'

'Thanks sergeant. Let me know if I can be of any help. Who's going to tell his poor mother? She's had more than enough tragedy in her lifetime.' Peter's father queried.

'Ah! It won't be pleasant. There's certainly no joy in it. Me and the constable will do that after they've verified the death and removed the body and I've cleared the bridge. It would be good 'though, if Mrs Devereau would pay the kid's mother a visit sometime this evening. The poor dear will need a sympathetic shoulder to cry on.' As Devereau struggled up the bank to the roadway, he passed the ambulance officers making their way, stretcher in hand, to collect Aadje's remains. Peter, convulsed with sobs of grief, with one arm around his father's neck and head on his shoulder, closed his eyes tight to quarantine his frail body from the despair that wracked him to the core. 'Arthur, if it's alright with you, I'll have Constable Allison move your truck from the bridge so that people can cross. Will you be okay to get home, or do you want us to help you out?'

'No. I think I can manage,' Arthur responded. 'Good. I'll catch up with you in a day or two for a little talk. Although, it won't take too long, I need to make my report. Still, I know what happened here,' stressed O'Reilly. 'My biggest problem is breaking the news to the lad's mother. I've got to get to Mrs Kuiper before dark and before some big mouth puts his foot in it,' declared the sergeant. The ambulance, with its grim cargo dressed in the robes of the departed, left for the mortuary. The sergeant, with his constable's help, cleared the bridge and prepared himself for the distressing task of visiting Mrs Kuiper in Jackson's Road to, as gently as he could, tell Aadje's mother the news that her son won't be coming home.

The abject horror on Anki Kuiper's face when she opened the door on Sgt O'Reilly and his constable is embossed on their memories for ever. Shaking, she choked out. 'It's Aadje, isn't it? What's happened? Where is he?'

'We have some bad news Mrs Kuiper, can we come in?' Aadje's mum, wringing her apron as she went, led them down the passage to her sparse kitchen. Taking a seat at the kitchen table and distractedly playing with a toy truck as its centre piece, O'Reilly broke the grim news. Mrs Kuiper, convulsed with sorrow and anguish, sobbed uncontrollably and collapsed onto the floor. Moans of grief and anger resonated through the kitchen. Plaintiff cries of, 'why?' came up from the floor as the two policemen, as gently as they could, lifted Anki back onto her seat. With Anki's head collapsed in her arms resting on the table, O'Reilly turned to his constable and said. 'Quick. Go and see if Mrs Deverau can come over, and, while you're at it, go to the hospital and get a nurse out here right away. This poor lady needs a woman's shoulder to cry on.' Bolting out the door, more in relief than mission, the constable fired up the police car and in a cloud of dust, was gone. O'Reilly, not knowing what to do, could only pat her shoulder and repeat. 'There. There. I know it hurts, but things will get better. You'll see.' O'Reilly, while an experienced policeman, could never come to grips with reporting a death to loved ones and always chided himself over his failure to offer any more comfort and solace than useless platitudes. He would be relieved when someone else arrived to take from him the mantle of a burden from which he brooked no pleasure, and at a time when he was most lost for words. Usually, in these circumstances, family arrived to invade his space and allow him to beat a hasty retreat. Tragically, Anki had no family to comfort her in the hour of her need, and where her only support came from the local constabulary and the company of comparative strangers.

Having got Peter home and explained the grisly outcome to his wife, they put him to bed and sat with him while he sobbed tears of torment. They talked of all things in a vain attempt to mitigate even a smidgeon of grief and, through trauma induced exhaustion, Peter fell into a fitful sleep. A sleep interrupted only by the nightmares that haunted his restlessness and filled the room with screams of tumult and suffering. 'No. No. Aadje come back,' Peter groaned, as he fitfully wrestled with his demons and anguish. The Devereau's kept a silent watch by Peter's bedside, while his mother gently caressed his head with the back of her hand. A loud knock on the door startled them from their vigil and fleetingly shook their mind from Peter's dark curtain of pain. Devereau on welcoming the constable, asked how everything was going?

'Not good,' replied Constable Allison. 'She's taking it very badly, the poor thing. Sgt O'Reilly was wondering if Mrs Devereau could come over straight away. The poor woman has no family and needs the help that we can't give her. The sergeant and me are all at sea and out of our depth when it comes to this sort of thing. I'm goin' up to the hospital to get a nurse. She needs something to help her sleep. Can Mrs Devereau go on up please? Sgt O'Reilly is on his own and really struggling,' beseeched the disconsolate constable, experiencing this type of crisis for the first time in his short career.

'What is it Bill?' Devereau heard his wife call.

'Anki is in a really bad way and they'd like you to go across and see if you can help the poor woman.'

'Of course I can, but what about Peter?'

'I'll be here to keep an eye on him while you're gone. I know it's not easy, but it'd be good if you could.'

'Oh. Dear. I don't have anything to take. I can't go empty handed.'

'Darling, believe me, the last thing Anki will want is something to eat, but take some tea and milk just in case she has none. Take the Ford. Peter will be okay with me. Come home when you think it's right,' Devereau said, with little enthusiasm and no joy. He was unsure of his fatherly capacities when left alone with a son who clearly needed the tender embrace of a mother at times like this. Still, he knew Mrs Kuiper's circumstances were far more dire and pressing. The constable thanked the Devereau's, took his leave and made haste for the hospital.

Devereau, overwhelmed with emotion, sat at the foot of Peter's bed and tenderly watched his son's restless endeavours to find peace in deep sleep. He prayed that Peter would journey through his troubles and emerge without the stigma of guilt and anger. He felt deeply sorry for Mrs Kuiper and wished he could make everything right again. 'Time is all we've got,' reasoned Devereau, as he nodded off in his none too comfortable perch that doubled as a chair. Awakened by a distant voice, Devereau slowly realised his son was calling him and asking for a drink and something to eat.

'A good sign,' thought Devereau as he scuttled off to the kitchen. 'With lots of talking we may just get Peter through this,' he mumbled, more in hope than optimism. He was sitting talking to a tearful Peter when he heard the family Ford crunch its way up the gravel driveway and herald his wife's return. Alice explained that she spent a lot of time talking to Anki and consoling her with copious quantities of tea and sympathy.

'She's in a bad way, but was a little more accepting when I left. A nurse from the hospital gave her something to help her sleep and that nice Mr Murphy called in and said he'd keep an eye on her.' Devereau smiled at the mention of Tom Murphy's name, for little did his wife know his track record for recycling.

'What is adding to Anki's anxiety and misery,' Mrs Devereau explained, 'is that she has next to no savings to give her son a decent funeral. She is beside herself with worry and sorrow. Gee. Bill. What can we do to make sure the poor kid has a proper burial? My heart bleeds for Anki and I haven't stopped crying since I got to her place and it really upset me when she told me of her money problems.'

'Yeah, it's not right. We owe it to Peter to give his friend the best send-off we can and his poor mother deserves at least a half way decent break in life. Right now, we're all grieving and Anki needs all the help she can get. Tomorrow I'll see what I can sort out with Bromwich and the Cemetery Trust. I might be able to at least come to some arrangement for the kid's funeral where most of the cost is taken care of. We've just got to make sure Peter is comforted so he can get over his loss and the feeling that he is responsible for what happened. Between you and I dear, we'll make it happen,' was Devereau's warm, but determined response.

'That'd be wonderful Bill. I might be able to swing the Country Women's Association into putting on a supper after the funeral. I reckon there won't be a problem with that. The CWA are always doing that sort of thing.'

The day broke hot as January days do in Bowater. Leaving Peter in the care of his mother, Devereau, with the zeal of a missionary, walked to Bromwich's funeral parlour and explained the dire circumstances confronting Mrs Kuiper. Grief, for Alan Bromwich, was stock in trade. He was sympathetic enough to offer the burial as cheaply as possible without compromising on respect for the dead young boy. He had a casket in storage, taking up space, that he would donate and he would also ask staff to work on the day as a favour to him. 'In the spirit of goodwill and to make their boss happy,' he laughed. 'Paupers are just dumped on the fringes of the cemetery and I make a claim for expenses. This funeral is a little different if the kid's going to have a proper burial. I'll do some shuffling in that regard after things have quieted a little,' winked Bromwich, warming to a conspiracy of his own creation. Mr Bromwich also pointed out that he needed to visit Mrs Kuiper to sort out funeral arrangements.

'While it is never a pleasant experience, it needs to be done. I will be happy to put her mind at rest and let her know we'll deliver a simple, but nice funeral for Aadje. The body was released this morning and it's being embalmed as we speak. His mother might like a viewing,' observed the funeral director. 'Do you reckon she'll want notices in the paper?'

'I doubt it, but ask her. We should let people know of the funeral arrangements at least. There may be some who would like to farewell the kid. In any case, I'll take care of that,' promised Devereau. 'Besides, the whole tragedy will be front page in the next *Bugle,* which'll more than likely blame the Council for risking lives by not making the bridge safe and O'Reilly for not stopping them,' sighed Devereau, lamenting the tragic turn of events.

'What about the burial plot? That's one area I can't help with, and don't forget the grave digger,' reminded Mr Bromwich.

'That's okay. I'm looking into that. The President of the Cemetery Trust owes me a favour or two. I might have to leverage his heart and mind for a little bit of charity.'

'I'll leave all that with you Bill. I'll catch up with Mrs Kuiper tomorrow to sort out the arrangements the best I can. I'll let her know her son will be buried next to his father. You reckon you can make that happen, Bill?'

'Yeah. Some way or other,' Devereau answered, more in hope than affirmation.

Back in his office, Devereau called to Millie and let her know he was off to see Martin Squires of the Cemetery Trust at his haberdashery store.

'I'll be gone for about an hour if anyone's looking for me,' directed Devereau as he walked out the door. 'Oh! By the way, I need to see Andy when I get back. Millie, can you let him know.'

The meeting with Squires of the Cemetery Trust went more smoothly than Devereau dare imagine. Its President had heard of the tragic events on the town's vibrant grapevine and, grasping Mrs Kuiper's parlous circumstances, agreed to spirit the burial plot over to her. 'By the time anyone wakes up to the shuffle, it'll be far too late. Clerical errors happen all the time,' he mused. Devereau just smiled at the Trust's new-found creativity and charitable largesse.

'Ah! I know what you're thinking Mr Devereau. God works in mysterious ways. I also wish to thank you for giving my nephew a job with the Council road gang. I haven't forgotten, and I appreciated what you did for him. He just couldn't handle working indoors and was useless when he worked for me. Much to my sister's consternation, haberdashery wasn't for him.'

'It was my pleasure Martin. But you really need to thank Andrew Dawson. He found a place for him on the roads. By the way, what about the grave digger? Devereau questioned.

'Still, I know you pushed it and I'm grateful for what you did for my sister's boy. Don't worry about the grave digger Bill. I'll take care of that. *Six Foot* McFadden is a good bloke and he'll understand when I let him know that, as a personal favour, I would like him to prepare the grave without charge.

'*Six Foot*,' queried a bemused and confused Devereau.

'Yeah! Arthur McFadden is known around the traps as *Six Foot*, and it's got nothing to do with his height.' A whimsical smile creased Deverau's face as it dawned on him the morbid significance of the moniker. 'I'm getting slow in my old age,' he thought with a chuckle.

'Thanks Martin. You have been more than understanding. I'll let the funeral home know that the grave site is under control and that the kid will be buried next to his father and sister.'

'That's okay. Bromwich's people, in any case, will be in touch with me as they sort out the funeral arrangements. I'm just glad I could be of help.'

On his return, Andy Dawson was waiting. 'You know about the kid who was drowned yesterday?'

'Yes Bill. It's very sad and such a waste,' rued Dawson, with a shrug of his shoulders.

'The kid wanted to be a truck driver, you know. I would like one of our trucks to lead the funeral cortege to the cemetery as a fitting gesture to the lad. It would be a meaningful mark of respect for a young bloke who never got to drive his own truck.'

'That's easy Bill. I'll organise it. Do we know when the funeral is?'

'We'll know tomorrow or the next day. I'll give you the details as soon as I find out.'

On his arrival home, Devereau was met by his wife at the door who was waiting for him to finish work. Alice Devereau was anxious to visit Mrs Kuiper with some food and words of comfort. As she left, Devereau asked her to let Mrs Kuiper know that the funeral won't cost her a shilling and that he was working on sorting out the costs. Devereau made his way to his son's room to check on his well-being and found him disconsolate, but open and communicative. Devereau smiled and silently praised his wife for her patience and healing 'I'm a lucky man and Anki is in good hands,' he thought. Calling his son, he asked Peter to come out to the shed with him and help with the Indian Scout. While Devereau enjoyed the quiet time with his new pride and joy, this time was more a ploy to spend time with Peter and, as part of the healing process, take his mind of his sad loss.

'One day, this thing of beauty will be yours son. When I can no longer ride her, she'll belong to you.'

'But dad, with my legs, I'll never be able to ride that big bike properly.'

'I know it's a bit hard right now Peter, but your legs will get stronger as you get older and you'll be able to engage the foot clutch. The gear change is hand operated. Just chuck your crutches into the sidecar and off you go. I've got no doubt you'll be strong enough to manage the beast,' Devereau cajoled.

'Gee. I hope so dad. I'd like that. I wish Aadje was here to see my bike,' said Peter, as he broke down in a flood of tears. With his arm draped over his son's shoulder, Devereau, now thinking it wasn't such a good idea to have Peter look over his bike, guided his son back to his room.

'Why did it have to happen to Aadje? He was good to me dad. I miss him so bad,' was Peter's anguished cry as they headed back inside.

'I know Peter. But, we can never understand why these things happen. We only know how. Aadje is in a better place with his dad and little sister and we should be happy about that,' was the best advice he could muster, immediately regretting the use of 'happy' in his words of comfort to a son struggling with his loss. Peter though, looking up at his father, felt a little more at peace than at any time since Aadje's fateful leap.

Mrs Devereau arrived home unexpectedly buoyed by her visit to Anki. Harrowing as it was, the two women had talked all things children and, while she went into stress and hyperventilated at times, she was slowly coming to an acceptance of Aadje's death and of the tragedies that had visited her far too often. While at Mrs Kuiper's, the Reverend Mitchell and Father Madden paid a visit of consolation and healing. 'I didn't think the family were Catholic,' questioned Devereau, when told of their visit.

'They're not, but Father Madden was so touched by Anki's plight that he came with the Reverend Mitchell and offered his condolences. They each gave Anki ten shillings from the church poor box to help out with funeral costs. At first, she refused to accept their kind gifts, but I talked her into taking the money. She took it with tears streaming down her face. The poor dear, she didn't look well. The Reverend Mitchell, his name's Clarence I think, told Mrs Kuiper not to worry about the service. He said he'd be privileged to do it and would arrange for an organist and some flowers. He told her it would be the Methodist Church's honour to help out in her time of need. Mr Murphy called in while I was there to offer his support and when I left the three of them were helping Anki through her grief and consoling her with their kindness, sympathy and love of God,' explained Alice Devereau, choking back tears of pain and suffering.

'That's good, darling. You did well. She might just get through this personal crisis with plenty of help from all of us,' prayed Devereau. 'Oh, well. We'll see what tomorrow brings,' were Devereau's last words, as he and his wife headed off to check on Peter, wish him good night and retire for the evening.

The paperwork on Bill Devereau's desk had piled up, neglected, on his desk over the past couple of days while he helped sort out the funeral for the Kuiper boy. Millie had prioritised the urgent material and positioned it right under his nose. He was busily ploughing through the signing of documents relating to audit returns, invoices, procurement bills, tenders and pressing Council reports when he was alerted by a gentle tapping on his office door.

'Come in,' Devereau invited. Standing before him was a tall, well-built and tanned young man of about thirty-five. Dressed in the blue singlet, blue shorts and heavy lace up boots that defined his class and status, the young man removed his weather clubbed and sweat stained hat and said, 'G'day sir. I'm Arthur McFadden. The Cemetery Trust use me as its grave digger. Mr Squires saw me last night about the kid. I'll do a nice job Mr Devereau. That young fellow helped me fill in a grave not so long ago and it's the least I can do to help out. He seemed like a good lad.'

'He was Arthur, and thank you for offering to help out. His mum, I'm sure, will be grateful.'

'It's the least I can do. Do you think it would be alright if I led the funeral procession with me truck? The kid told me he loved trucks and wanted to drive one when he grew up.'

'I've already organised to have a Council truck lead, but why don't we make it two. You lead the way, my truck can follow. I'll talk to Bromwich so they understand what we're planning.'

'Sounds good to me,' said Arthur. 'I'd better get goin' now. I got work to do. It's been good meeting you Mr Devereau.'

'Thanks again Arthur. But, please call me Bill. I appreciate your help. Catch you later. I'll sort out the trucks with the funeral home when, sometime today, I catch up with Mr Bromwich.'

On hearing his door close, Devereau once more returned to the paperwork that now lay strewn across his desk. He was having trouble concentrating. His thoughts returned to his son and hoped he was coping with his sorrow.

'Poor Anki. How must she be feeling right now,' he wondered. As the day wore on, Devereau became increasingly despondent with worry over Peter and Aadje's mother, who he knew would be wracked with distress and an empty loneliness.

Mr Bromwich arrived as promised and filled Devereau in on the funeral arrangements that he, while nurturing a distraught Mrs Kuiper, had fashioned with her and the Reverend Clarence Mitchell.

'Two o'clock next Monday at the Methodist Church in Beacon Street. The wake will be in the Church Hall at four o'clock. I understand the Church auxiliary and the local CWA ladies are taking care of the afternoon tea. Because of that, I've worded up one of my attendants to warn Barry O'Dowd off and tell him to stay away from the funeral.'

'Why would you want to do that? I would have thought the more people farewelling the young bloke the better it would be for his mum,' queried Devereau, taken aback by the mere hint of turning anyone away from the burial.

'Don't you know about O'Dowd, Bill? We call him *Bury'em Barry* because he has a bad habit of turning up at funerals, even of people he's never heard of, just to get a free feed.'

'The cunning devil,' was all an incredulous Devereau could offer, his mind swimming in disbelief at the guile of the crafty.

'You did well with the Cemetery Trust Bill. It will be a fitting send off for the lad. I think his mother will be pleased that she is able see her son have a decent burial.' Bromwich went on to explain that Mrs Kuiper would like to view the body tomorrow evening.

'I think she's up to it. Clarence will be with her for support if she needs it. And the way things are, she'll need all the support we can give her. What about your boy, Bill? Do you think he would like to come along and pay his respects?'

'I dunno, Mr Bromwich. I don't think so. It might upset him too much. Alice has been working on his grief and I don't want to risk setting him back.'

'I understand Bill. But, often viewing the body and being able to say a personal goodbye sometimes helps with the healing you know.'

'Look, I'll have a little talk to him and his mother tonight and sort it out from there. What time is the viewing?'

'Seven o'clock. Don't worry, the lad will look peaceful and it might help your young bloke.'

'I'll see how it goes when I get home,' mumbled Devereau quietly, wishing it would all go away.

As Mr Bromwich took his leave, he turned, 'I almost forgot, Clarence's Church auxiliary is arranging some flowers for the service. I think that's very nice of them.'

'That's great. I'm really pleased people have seen fit to rally around Mrs Kuiper in her time of need. She can do with all the comfort and sympathy she can get.'

Alice Devereau busied herself with household chores while keeping a close watch on Peter. She was relieved to see that he, while occasionally lapsing into a flood of misery, was bearing up reasonably well to the loss of his friend. She knew Aadje's death had greatly troubled her son and that his emotions spiralled into a black emptiness at the very thought of his friend being no longer with him. Peter cried a lot, but he was eating and could talk, with some encouragement, about Aadje's death and what he had witnessed just three days before.

'I think he'll be okay with time,' Mrs Devereau consoled herself, through her own veil of anxiety. 'Time heals all wounds,' was her new, if unoriginal, dictum. She knew Peter felt a little better when, together with a sprig of flowers from the Devereau garden, they made their way to the apex of Curlin's Bridge and threw them into the river below.

As they watched the blooms glide north on the river's current, Peter, tears cascading down his reddened cheeks, bid his mate farewell. His mother, arms over his shoulder, whispered that Aadje was in a better place and that he wouldn't want his friend upset by his leaving.

Deep in concern for Mrs Kuiper, Alice Devereau was laying the finishing touches to tidying up the lounge room when a knock at the door startled her back to the here and now. Standing on the verandah, in front of the fly wire door, were three sun tanned young lads.

'Hello there,' was Alice Devereau's first reaction. 'How can I help you?'

'Sorry to disturb you Mrs Devereau. I'm Jerome Gavin and this is Ginger and Spike,' said Blackie, pointing to each of them in turn. 'We're wondering if we could talk to Peter. We want to tell him we're feelin' bad about what happened.' As realisation dawned, Alice Devereau asked. 'You're Blackie aren't you?'

'Yes Mrs Devereau, and we're really sorry for what happened.'

'It's a bit late for that now Jerome. It has ended all too badly. I'll see if Peter will talk to you. He's very upset you know.'

'I know Mrs Devereau, but do you think Peter would see us even for a minute?' Leaving the three boys on the verandah, uncomfortable, shuffling with eyes downcast, Mrs Devereau made her way to Peter's bedroom to announce his visitors. Reluctant to see them, he allowed his mother to convince him otherwise.

'It won't hurt to talk to them Peter. I'm here.'

'Alright,' Peter whispered as he locked his callipers, grabbed his crutches and made his way to the front veran-dah. On seeing Peter at the door, Blackie blushed and started to speak.

'Look Peter, we're really sorry for what happened to Aadje. It wasn't s'posed to be like this. We didn't mean it. It was just a bit of fun. We didn't hate him. He was just there and didn't fight back,' Blackie blurted out in a voice that bespoke of genuine regret and guilt.

'Yeah! Well you hurt Aadje and you had no right to treat him mean like you did. He was a good friend. He took care of me and helped me get around.'

'I know Peter. I'm truly sorry and we want to make it up to you. You'll see. We'll look after you?'

'What. Just like you looked after Adje. You know he only had his mum and me. You were nasty and cruel. It wasn't fair.'

'This time it will be different,' mumbled Blackie, casting a rueful glance over his sorry accomplices. Nodding in uni-son, they once more cast their eyes downward and uttered nothing.

'It's all your fault he's gone. He wanted to be just like you. He wanted to be looked up to. He wanted to prove he was as good as you. That's why he jumped. He wanted you to like him. That's all he wanted,' rasped Peter, through the blur of tears flooding his eyes and cascading down his cheeks. Taken aback by Peter's verbal assault, and in obvious distress,

Blackie could only add. 'We're really sorry Peter. Don't be mad with us.'

At this point, Mrs Devereau, who had been standing behind Peter in the doorway, jumped in with, 'alright, boys. As you can see, Peter's very upset. It might be best if you went home and came back a few days down the track. Things might be better then.' As the boys scuttled through the front gate, Mrs Devereau began to doubt the wisdom in allowing the boys to talk to Peter. At the time she felt a whiff of sympathy for the feelings of the three bullies who had played a pretty big part in the tragedy they were all now living with. After helping Peter back to his room, she sat on the edge of his bed until the tears stopped flowing and he seemed to have returned to some semblance of calm.

'Oh, dear,' she thought. 'Will this darkness and sorrow never end.'

The viewing went as expected. Anki broke down into inconsolable grief. The Reverend Clarence Mitchell was there to provide comfort and support. His clerical collar, his badge of office and calling, gave him the credentials for healing, and all in God's name. Anki held on to the casket so tight her knuckles whitened as she wailed. 'Aadje. Aadje come back. I love you. I need you. Why did you leave me? What sort of God took you from me?' With anger rising to boiling she looked, through tear stained mascara, at the reverend and pounding him on the chest screamed at the man of cloth. 'Your God killed my husband and my little girl and he finished me off by taking my only son. What sort of God is that?' The Reverend Mitchell, hugged her to his bosom and, in the only words of comfort he could muster, called on a higher authority.

'God works in mysterious ways and He'll guide you through your anguish. Aadje has gone to the Kingdom of Heaven and he shall not want,' were his words of kindness as he gently led Mrs Kuiper to the door. Turning abruptly, Anki broke free of Mitchell's embrace and bounded back to Aadje's lifeless body. Through cascading tears and hysteria, she cried. 'Goodbye my son. I love you and will always miss you. How can I live without you? Farewell my beautiful boy. Say hello to your dad and sister for me. We'll all be together again shortly Aadje. You're a good boy and I love you son.' Then, in the gentle arms of the Reverend, she disappeared through the chapel's frosted double doors. Sobs of grief echoing into the evening heralded a silence even Alan Bromwich found eerie. Signalling to one of his assistants, he instructed in barely a whisper. 'Duck around to the hospital and see if a nurse can run over to Mrs Kuiper's. She's in a very bad way and even Clarence, with all his skill and experience might need some help. Although, I think he's got a couple of church ladies to help out tonight, the poor woman is going to need something to help her sleep.'

As his assistant broached the evening air, and as Bromwich was about to close the coffin, the sound of a car pulling up on the gravel driveway gained his undivided attention.

'Ah. This'll be Bill Devereau,' he thought. 'They must have decided it would be okay for his son to view the body.

Peter only spent a few minutes with Aadje's lifeless form. Standing back a little, his mother and father, concern etched into their foreheads, watched their son shuffle over to the coffin and propping a crutch against Aadje's bed of death, he farewelled his friend. 'Goodbye Aadje. I'll miss you so much. We had a lotta fun together and you always looked after me.' With tears running freely, he touched his friend on his cold, ashen cheek and growled. 'Why did you have to leave me. You were my only friend. I didn't want you to jump. Don't worry, I'll take care of your ferrets and look after your mum.' He then just stood transfixed beside the casket, convulsed with bouts of sobbing. Peter, staring at his lost mate at peace in his bed of blue satin, began shaking with anguish. Growing ever more concerned, Mrs Devereau stepped forward, put her arm around his shoulder and, in a voice stroked with tenderness, whispered. 'I think it's time to go now Peter. Aadje needs some peace and quiet. He'll be pleased you said g'day and waved him a goodbye. Why don't we go home now and get some rest?'

Peter allowed himself to be manoeuvred out of the chapel and into the family car. 'Son, are you okay?' Devereau struggled with the only words he could muster, knowing full well the answer to his own question. For, he was acutely aware that it would be quite a while before Peter could even begin to feel alright.

'I'm glad I went to see Aadje dad. I wanted to say goodbye. I miss him already,' Peter commented, tears forming rivulets as they ran down his cheeks. Devereau, turning to his wife declared. 'He'll be alright love. He's strong.' Mrs Devereau, who had once more doubted her own wisdom in allowing Peter to view Aadje's body, rejoined. 'I just hope we've done the right thing Bill.' But, Peter, she realised wanted to come, and she felt keeping him away would be more hurtful than bringing him along. 'Time will tell.' She thought, fighting back tears through tightly closed eyes. With that the Ford pulled into the driveway of the California Bungalow they called home. As Devereau alighted from the car and helped Peter out, he mused, 'Tomorrow's another day. Let's see what it brings.' With that, they all headed inside to the comfort of a home that, albeit temporarily at least, shielded them from the sting of a world most unforgiving. Alone in the company of their own anguish, they would somehow cope, and embrace happiness once more.

Requiem's Dark Shadow

Bowater's St Luke's Methodist Church, built in 1863, bathed in the glow of a hot January sun, sat in all its spiritual glory. The white cross that dominated its hipped roof symbolised salvation and redemption. The sun beat down a relentless tattoo from a cloudless sky that tore the heart out of its gravel driveway and stressed the landscape to the kernel. A concrete path, channelled between a row of wilted roses herded parishioners to a vestibule that opened into a nave with vistas of stained glass and harsh wooden pews, polished by history and the shuffling of worshippers. The pulpit that had presided over past glories and much sorrow, tyrannised the small church with all the authority vested in it by God's pious flock. Beside the church sat a black hearse, with its attendants bedecked in dark suits and black top hats standing mute at its tail gate. Keeping it company were two flat-bed trucks, one carrying the emblem of the Shire on its logoed door, while the other sported a large floral wreath centred on its pristine tray. Inside, the casket, adorned with flowers of many colours, was laid out before the pulpit. A toy truck atop the coffin spoke of dreams lost and ambition unfulfilled. Seventeen mourners, caressed by the strains of 'Amazing Grace', had gathered to witness Aadje's journey into the after-life. Anki, in a state of near collapse, was comforted by Alice Devereau and Tom Murphy, who with Peter and his father, occupied the front pew. Mr Kwong, on entering the church and fighting back the tears welling inside him, made his way to the coffin and, placing his hands upon it, with bowed head recited in Mandarin what the grieving congregation assumed to be the sayings of *Confucius*. Mr Kwong, clearly struggling with his emotions, patted Peter gently on the shoulder as he passed and slid into a seat behind the other mourners. The pews, sparsely populated, creaked along with the discomfort of Mr Rae and Miss Everitt, Aadje's English teacher. Arthur McFadden, Bugsy Moran, Andy Dawson and Millie, who came along to support the Shire Secretary and his son filled the rest of the pew. Two young girls from Aadje's class, chaperoned by their mothers, had come to say a last goodbye as they farewelled him on his journey into immortality. Mrs Fuller and Mrs Keene, who sat at the back of the church, feeling most uncomfortable, had already done their best to comfort Anki with soothing words that meant little to her while suffering a tidal wave of woe. The organist, having exhausted her repertoire of hymns, was beginning to repeat her repertory when, at two o'clock on the dot, the Reverend Mitchell, glided through the tapestry curtain behind the pulpit. He ascended his eyrie and eyed his congregation of sweating despair. On cue, Mrs Blackney attacked her organ with renewed vigour and belted out the '*Lord's My Shepherd*', and, above the gentle sobs, the Minister welcomed all into the presence of God who in time of sorrow gives comfort and salvation. It was, he explained, his melancholy duty to farewell Aadje Geert Kuiper into the bounteous bosom of Jesus and to praise the life of a young man taken far too early from a loving mother and his friends. Reverend Clarence Mitchell described Aadje as a good boy who took care of his mum, ran washing around the streets and whose dream it was to become a truck driver. He doted on his mother and loved her dearly. He was a young man with love in his heart. Taken from our midst far too soon. 'We may ask why in God's name he chose Aadje to join Him in the Kingdom of Heaven. But, ours is not to reason why. God needed his talents and kindness more than us mere mortals. Aadje, son and friend, has gone to a better place.' With his head raised to the ceiling, the Reverend intoned, 'Blessed are they that mourn, for they shall be comforted. Let us pray.' The congregation, heads bowed, listened and mumbled in harmony as Mitchell recited the 'Lord's Prayer'

'For those who knew Aadje, we shall remember him always. Let us pray. Father in Heaven, we praise your name for all who finished this life loving and trusting you, for all the example of their lives, the life and grace you gave them, and the peace in which they rest. We praise you today for your servant Aadje Kuiper and for all that you did through him. Meet us in our sadness and fill our hearts with praise and thanksgiving for the sake of our risen Lord Jesus Christ. Amen.' Following readings from *John* and *Revelation,* the Reverend eulogised that Aadje would be deeply missed by all who knew and loved him. 'Mrs Kuiper invites you all to refreshments in the Church Hall following her son's laying to rest.' To the strains of 'Nearer my God', the two attendants, who, having entered by a side door and free of their top hats, were joined by Bill Devereau, Tom Murphy, Arthur McFadden and Peter Moran and hoisted Aadje's mortal remains onto their shoulders.

'Lord, now lettest thy servant depart in peace, according thy word. Let the light be witness to God's everlasting love,' were the Reverend's last words as the coffin made its way slowly down the aisle of the church to the waiting hearse. A journey accompanied by the organist enjoying her lot and belting out 'Abide with Me' and 'How Sweet the Name of Jesus'. Anki, distraught, was propped up by Mrs Devereau as she sobbed her way behind Aadje as he began his eternal journey into immortality. One by one, the mourners filed in behind the casket and mournfully followed it out into the bright sunlight.

The Reverend, who had followed directly behind the coffin, stopped at the door of the vestibule and thanked the mourners for their attendance and proffered words of comfort. The small knot of mourners stood around, shuffling in their muted conversation as the funeral home attendants closed the tail gate on Aadje's last journey.

'Did you organise the surprise for me? Devereau asked Andy Dawson who was, with Millie, hovering nearby. 'Sure enough did Bill. I'll drop it around after all this is over,' was Dawson's response. Mr Kwong, visibly distressed, approached Peter and in a voice wracked with despair, said hello to him and offered words of comfort and friendship.

'Are you going to the cemetery, Mr Kwong?' asked a disconcerted Devereau. 'I would like to, but I've only got my bicycle and it'd never get me there in time. I'll ride out after it's all over and give my regards to my friend Aadje,' was the Chinaman's response, choking back tears.

'You can come with me in the truck, if you want. But I've got work to do out there so I won't be able to bring you back unless you want to wait for me. But that won't help if you're going to the wake,' Arthur McFadden explained. 'I would like that. I won't be coming back for the wake. I'd be outta place,' Mr Kwong responded with a bow. 'Well, you wouldn't be, but it's up to you. You'll have your bike out there and you can please yourself what you do after the burial service,' observed McFadden, fully grasping the Chinaman's trepidation in attending the wake. Having tethered Chen Kwong's bicycle onto the flat-bed next to the wreath, McFadden and Kwong made their way to the cabin where *Six Foot* fired up the Bedford and let it idle.

Mrs Kuiper, Alice Devereau comforting her with all the tenderness she could muster, was led to the Devereau car and helped into the back seat. Sobs were all that consumed Anki as the procession, led by the two trucks, set off for the cemetery. Peter broke down in sympathy with Aadje's mother and cried the tears that only sadness brings. The procession came to a halt at the very apex of Curlin's Bridge where Arthur, assisted by his fellow truck driver and Mr Kwong, respectfully dispatched the wreath into the waters of the Daraleet some thirty feet below. As they watched their tribute in hues sublime floating on the water's embrace and slowly drifting to journey's end, they all bade Aadje farewell and followed the symbol of their respect out of sight as it went under the bridge. Once more on the move, the cortege of eight vehicles made their way to Bowater's cemetery, four miles up the road.

Aadje's coffin was placed gently next to his open grave site and to the right of his dad. His sister occupied pride of place on the left of their father's burial place. The Reverend Mitchell, with mourners gathered around a sobbing Mrs Kuiper, committed Aadje to his final resting place with readings from the scripture and words of encouragement and comfort. Mitchell recited poetry to sooth the pain of death.

> '*Although our grief is deep and raw,*
> *Although our pain is great,*
> *I know that you are still with us,*
> *I know that you will wait.*'

Scanning the knot of mourners, the Reverend Mitchell, eyes closed, began. 'We are gathered here to lay the mortal remains of our dearly beloved Aadje and entrust him into

God's care. May He bless him and keep him safe forever. Blessed are the meek, for they shall inherit the earth.' Hands clasped in prayer and looking to the Heavens, the Minister concluded with a prayer he hoped would give Anki Kuiper some relief from the pain wracking her very being.

> *'Eternal rest, grant unto them o'Lord,*
> *And let perpetual light shine on them,*
> *May the souls of the faithful departed,*
> *Through the mercy of God, rest in peace.'*
> 'Amen.'

With that the coffin was lowered to its final home and the mourners, led by his mother, threw petals of love and despair onto the casket some six feet below. Anki, now distraught and inconsolable, stood transfixed at the graves of her family before collapsing onto the ground in a torrent of tears. Peter, paralysed with anguish, dropped one of his crutches and clung to his father for support. Helping Anki into their car, the Devereau's made the slow and painful journey back to the church hall for refreshments. As all the mourners made their way out through the cemetery's ornate wrought iron gates, festooned with icons of the religious, silence once more invaded God's little acre. Peace and serenity had again resumed their rightful place as beacons of the blessed and protectors of the departed.

A lone figure, who had been standing a little way off under a peppercorn tree during the internment, approached the grave and made a sign of the cross while reciting a quiet prayer. Sifting some fine dirt through his manicured fingers, he sprinkles it over the coffin below. As he wanders off, he runs into Arthur and Kwong.

'G'day Father Madden. I didn't expect to see you out here,' McFadden mused.

'Hello my son. I just wanted to show my respect. The young lad was not of my faith, but we're all God's little children and my heart bleeds for his poor mother.'

'Yeah! It's tough alright. I hope she gets through this.'

'Clarence will make sure she's okay. I thought you were part of the funeral Arthur. Aren't you going to the wake?'

'Nah! I wanna finish here. I owe the young bloke and I want to fill in his grave. It's only right. I only live up the road from his mum. I'll call in sometime soon and see if she needs anything. Although, I see, Tom Murphy seems to have taken her under his wing.'

As the grave digger began his forlorn task, helped by Chen Kwong, the priest, with a smile, queried. 'You got another shovel? I'll give you a hand my son.'

'You're not dressed for it Father. We'll be alright.' Father Madden, with the raise of an eyebrow, removed his clerical collar and jettisoned his jacket. 'I am now. Let's get started.'

While the grave digger and his two companions busied themselves with the task at hand, the shadows of the gravestones lengthened in harmony with the afternoon sun and an eerie tranquillity once more descended upon the souls of God's chosen ones.

The wake, attended by a small number of sombre faced mourners, was heavy with desolation. The refreshments, spread with appetising splendour, saw a welter of sandwiches, scones and cream cakes. With Bury'em Barry conspicuous in his absence, all went largely uneaten by people lost in grief and discomfort. Not knowing what to say to Anki, or how to say it, they chose to congregate in little rosettes of their own choosing and communicate in muffled whispers. Mr Murphy and Alice Devereau comforted Anki the best they could. Guests, one at a time, on their way out stopped to offer words of condolences, with Mrs Fuller putting her arm around Anki and wishing things were better.

'When you feel up to it, I'll bring some washing around. And, I'll have others do the same,' were her parting words. As the last mourners left, Mrs Devereau thanked her friends in the CWA for providing, with the church auxiliary, afternoon tea and allowed Mr Murphy to take Anki home to her portal of sorrow. With a comforting arm draped over her shoulder, Murphy said in a voice mellowed gentle with concern, 'come on Anki, let's go home. I'll look after you. I'll always be around to help. Don't you worry about a thing.'

The Deverau's made their way home in the solitude of their own thoughts. They were met at the gate by Andy Dawson gently cradling a Border Collie pup in his arms. The black and white bundle of fidget was to be a gift for Peter from his mother and father to help him get over the loss of his friend. With eyes widening through pools of tears, Peter asked if the dog was his.

'It's yours Peter. She's a girl and we thought you might like it for company. Dad can take her for walks until you can manage her with your crutches,' announced his mother. Smiling broadly, Peter sat on the verandah, unlocked his callipers and took his new-found friend in his arms. With the Border Collie licking his face, his mother asked. 'What are you going to call her son?' Looking up at his mother, father and Andy Dawson, and, without a shadow of hesitation, Peter smiled, 'Towser. Aadje would like that.' While Peter fondled his pet of consolation, Alice Devereau let her husband know that she would visit Anki as often as need be. 'She hasn't got a lot of money and without Aadje to run washing around town, she'll find it hard to make ends meet on her widows' pension. She'll lose her Child Endowment too, you know. But we'll make sure she is alright and that nice Mr Murphy will take care of her until she can get back on her feet. Poor woman. What must it be like?'

Four days later, while Peter was sitting with Towser's head upon his leg, Jerome Gavin and Ginger arrived at his front fence. With fishing rods in hand, they were inviting Peter to go fishing with them. Mrs Devereau, not aware of the extent of his previous exploits with Aadje, expressed some concern for Peter's safety near water and, given the events of the past, was somewhat reluctant. Peter was unsure and now that he had a pup for company, he was reticent in joining Aadje's tormentors for the solitude of fishing. His mother, with a sigh and shrug of resignation, said. 'Oh. Go on son. It might be good for you and I think these boys really want to be friends and make it up to you.' As Peter locked his callipers and struggled to his feet, he heard his mother in a tone that spoke of a concern that carried a veiled threat, instructed. 'Jerome, you take care of my son around water. With his callipers he can't swim. You make sure you look after him and have him home before dinner. Towser will be fine with me son. She'll be right here until you get back.'

'We'll look after Peter. We'll take good care of him, Mrs Devereau,' the boys promised in unison. 'We can take the Collie. I'll handle its lead,' proffered Blackie.

'I think, for this time fellows, we'll keep Towser here. She'll be better off with me and you'll have one less thing to worry about,' Mrs Devereau observed. The boys waited for Peter to make his ungainly passage to the front gate and walked either side, keeping pace with him, as they made their way down the jacaranda lined street and disappeared from view.

Bill Devereau, at his office desk, looked out at Bowater's bustling streetscape, with its rural idyll bathed in bright sunshine, and reflected on the tragedy that had left the blight of despair across a community divided. As anticipated, the *Bugle* used the tragedy to berate Council and the local police for decades of inaction relating to the safety of Curlin's Bridge, and in failing to deter young dare devils from risking body and soul by diving off its apex. For its part, the *Bugle* had been informed that the inquest into the boy's death was scheduled for some time in May. Devereau was quietly relaxed over the impending coronial inquiry. He had feared

Peter would be called to relive the whole calamity again. Sgt O'Reilly had already talked to Peter and reassured Devereau that, given it would be straight forward inquiry, Peter would, in all probability, not be required. Council affairs were once more consuming his energies and, when in his darker moments he reflected on the enemies he had made in the chamber and the power vested in the weight of numbers and privilege, he took solace in the dictum that *the dingo waits*. Peter had come to adore Towser and spent every available minute with her. He missed his friend terribly, but, while he still cried at the thought, was coming to grips with Aadje's passing. Peter would soon turn fourteen and Devereau hoped the passage of time would slowly expunge the grief and the guilt he felt over his mate's loss.

His lovely wife, with Mr Murphy's help, was taking care of Anki and nursing her through her haze of sorrow. Arthur McFadden had fashioned a nice cross for Aadje's grave site and the ladies' auxiliary were raising money to give Aadje a proper headstone. Mr Murphy takes Anki out to visit her son's grave and the Devereau's take Peter out to the cemetery whenever he wants to talk to his friend. With Towser keeping her distance, the ferrets found a new home and some fingers in the Devereau back yard and Peter occasionally goes fishing with Jerome and Ginger. Mr Kwong often pays Mrs Kuiper a visit with some fresh vegetables and regularly hawks his wares along River Road. Spending time with Peter, imparting words of wisdom, reminiscing of a time when Aadje's spirit roamed free and of a friend now gone.

Bowater, having chased the nymphs of happiness into the fig tree of grief, was once again embracing its soul.

'For Aadje, it was a bridge too high, but life would go on and requiem's dark shadow will soon be driven from misery's cruel landscape,' reflected a somewhat relaxed Devereau. Smiling broadly, he waxed lyrical and lectured his empty office, 'Arcadia, a lacerated soul cloaked in discord and draped in tragedy, had lost its lustre. Its resurrection will come. It must, for we know not for whom the river runs'.

THE END